# AN EARL FOR IRIS

ELLIE ST. CLAIR

♥ Copyright 2019 by Ellie St Clair - All rights reserved.

In no way is it legal to reproduce, duplicate, or transmit any part of this document in either electronic means or in printed format. Recording of this publication is strictly prohibited and any storage of this document is not allowed unless with written permission from the publisher. All rights reserved.

Respective authors own all copyrights not held by the publisher.

Facebook: Ellie St. Clair

Cover by AJF Designs

Do you love historical romance? Receive access to a free ebook, as well as exclusive content such as giveaways, contests, freebies and advance notice of pre-orders through my mailing list!

Sign up here!

**Also By Ellie St. Clair**

*Standalone*
Unmasking a Duke
Christmastide with His Countess

*Happily Ever After*
The Duke She Wished For
Someday Her Duke Will Come
Once Upon a Duke's Dream
He's a Duke, But I Love Him
Loved by the Viscount
Because the Earl Loved Me

Happily Ever After Box Set Books 1-3
Happily Ever After Box Set Books 4-6

*Searching Hearts*
Duke of Christmas

Quest of Honor
Clue of Affection
Hearts of Trust
Hope of Romance
Promise of Redemption

Searching Hearts Box Set (Books 1-5)

*The Unconventional Ladies*
Lady of Mystery
Lady of Fortune
Lady of Providence
Lady of Charade

*Blooming Brides*
A Duke for Daisy
A Marquess for Marigold
An Earl for Iris

# 1

**1813**

"And then, Mother walked into the guests' sitting room, finding two fully grown men rolling on the floor, well in their cups. With Father out, the next thing I knew, she was running into *our* own sitting room, as flustered as ever and—"

"Iris? Iris, there you are!"

When Millie's voice cut through her tale and into her consciousness, Iris turned away from the counter at the general store, where she was regaling her friends with the latest narrative from her family's inn. There had been many stories of interest from The Wild Rose Inn since a steady stream of men had come to stay with them, home from the war effort and either convalescing or hiding for one reason or another now that they were back on English soil. The many stories had only increased Iris' popularity among the other young people in town.

"One moment," she said with a smile to the two young women and the teenage boy who had gathered to listen to her. They were from just beyond the town's borders, in for supplies and the latest gossip to return home with.

"Millie!" she said, turning her attention to the girl, who had originally been close with Iris' oldest sister, Daisy. Since Daisy had married her duke and left home, however, Millie had become increasingly close with the other sisters as well. When Iris took in Millie's flustered appearance, her countenance became much more serious as her worry increased. "Whatever is the matter?"

"Can we go outside for a moment?"

Iris looked back at her audience and was disappointed in the thought of leaving them before finishing her story, but Millie looked so concerned that she nodded and followed her out the door onto the road, where the late summer air was thick with unexpected heat despite their proximity to the sea.

"I need your help," Millie said the moment they were out of earshot of any passersby.

"*My* help?"

Of the four Tavners sisters, Iris certainly wasn't the one most came to for help or advice. Of course, with Daisy and Marigold married and moved away, between Iris and Violet, she supposed she might be the more approachable one as Violet's head was always stuck in a book. Although, if anyone took the time to ask her, Violet actually typically provided a clear head and sound thoughts.

"Yes, your help. You are the perfect person to aid me."

"Very well. What can I do?"

It was actually kind of nice to be the one someone came to for help for once, and Iris determined she would do what she could to aid Millie.

"You know Father wants me to marry Ernest, the apothecary's son," Millie began.

*An Earl for Iris*

"Yes, I am aware," Iris said, wrinkling her nose at the thought. "You simply *cannot* marry the fool."

"Of course not," Millie said forlornly. "He is more self-absorbed than any person I have ever met, and when he looks at me I feel chills creeping down my back. Father doesn't understand these things, and is insistent, as he feels Ernest could provide me with a stable home."

"I suppose it is true that if he follows his father's profession, an apothecary *would* be able to provide for you."

"Unlike a fisherman."

Iris hadn't wanted to say it, but Millie was right. The man Millie loved, Burt Clarkson, would likely live near to poverty for the rest of his life. But Millie loved him, and to her, that was all that mattered.

"You are set on marrying Burt, are you not?"

"I am," Millie confirmed, though she didn't look particularly happy. "He has offered for me, but my father turned him down. Now Ernest has asked for my hand and my father agrees though I certainly do not. I cannot marry him, Iris, I simply cannot!"

"No one can force you to marry, Millie," Iris said, crossing her arms over her chest.

"He is my father. I am all he has in this world," Millie said, her brown eyes turning desperate. She was quite fair and pretty, and it was no wonder she had more than one man interested in her. "I cannot have him renounce me or turn from me, for then what would I do? No, I have thought of a better way."

"What is it?" Iris asked, curious now.

"We must convince Ernest that he is no longer interested in marrying me. What better way to do so than to turn his attention elsewhere?"

A sinking feeling filled Iris as she hesitated at first, but then had to ask, "And how would you do that?"

"By turning his affections toward you!"

"Oh." Iris swallowed hard.

"I know it is much to ask, Iris, but with just a bit of attention from you, I'm sure he would lose all interest in me. You're the most beautiful woman in town, everyone knows that, and he has made it abundantly clear to all that you would be his first choice. There's a dance in a few days' time. All you have to do is visit him at the apothecary's before that, flirt a little, dance with him that evening, and he will be smitten and forget all about me. Your father would never force you to marry someone you didn't want, not like mine. So, would you do it?"

Iris bit her lip. This was the last thing she wanted to agree to, and yet, she had said she would help Millie in whatever way she could.

"I..."

"You have no one else who has captured your affections, have you?" Millie asked suddenly. "For if so, I would never ask this of you."

Iris ducked her head for a moment. The truth was, there actually *was* someone who had captured her affections, as Millie put it. An image came into her mind of a man with light brown tousled hair, broad shoulders, and a smile so warm and charming it could melt the frozen ice of a lake in mid-winter.

But it didn't matter that he had her heart. That particular man was not for her, as he had made perfectly clear but two months ago when she had misread his signals and leaned in to kiss him. Thinking of it now filled her with horror once more at the embarrassment it had caused her, for she had been well and truly rejected. His heart was with another, and she would do well to remember it.

"There is no one," she said now, forcing a smile onto her face. "Sure, Millie, for you, I will do it."

"Oh, thank goodness," Millie said with relief, placing her hands on Iris' arm. "I knew I could count on you."

And, for a moment, Millie's gratitude was enough.

~

OR SO IRIS THOUGHT, until later that afternoon when she found herself within the apothecary's shop. She hadn't often been in here, for her sister Marigold had always seemed to be coming up with some concoction or another to treat their family's ailments.

But now that Marigold had moved near Cambridge with her husband, they had to once more rely on the apothecary should they require any particular treatments for ailments that might arise within the family or the boarders at their inn.

"Iris Tavners, how lovely to see you today," said Mr. Abernathy, the apothecary, as he looked at Iris overtop of his spectacles. "What seems to be the issue today?"

"I, ah, am actually here to see Ernest," she said, forcing a smile to her face, despite the loathing within her stomach. "Is he in?"

"Oh!" Mr. Abernathy said in surprise. "He is, actually. One moment."

As he scurried to the back of the shop, Iris turned to look around her at the rows of bottles upon the walls. Mrs. Abernathy gave her a wave from the corner, where she was currently sitting at a table filling some of the said bottles. Iris cringed. She could hardly imagine life wed to the apothecary. Perhaps if he was a decent man, it would be no issue, but Ernest—

"Iris!" he exclaimed as he came out of the back room, pushing through the swinging doors. "I hear you have inquired about me. I am pleased to finally hear it."

Ernest had come courting a year or two ago, and Iris had swiftly brushed him aside. He was far too arrogant for her liking. If she was being honest, Iris would have to admit that she far preferred a man who was more eager to sing *her* praises than his own.

"Yes, well—"

"It does make sense that the two of us should explore what could be with one another, does it not? You are, after all, the most beautiful girl in town, and therefore it makes perfect sense that we would make a match."

Goodness, she had done nothing but ask if he was within the shop and he practically had them married. This was too much. She couldn't—

"You were almost too late, you know," he said, leaning across the counter, whispering conspiratorially. "I am soon to be betrothed to another. Although, I imagine that is what lured you my way. I should have created such a scheme ages ago! Nothing a little jealousy won't cure."

As he laughed, Iris managed a weak smile. Every fiber within her body desired to flee, to leave him behind, but then she remembered Millie and her desperate plea. There was one thing Iris was not, and that was a coward.

She looked down for a moment before turning her gaze back up to Ernest from beneath her lashes, a practiced look that always seemed to work.

"How do you know that is why I am here, Ernest?" she asked, dipping her voice ever so slightly. "Perhaps I am simply here to ask your advice on a potion or two."

"Perhaps," he said with a shrug. "But I know better."

"You are too intelligent to fool. As it happens, there is to be a dance at the Johnsons' new barn in a few days' time," she said. "I was hoping you would save me a dance or two."

"That is a rather forward request, Iris."

She shrugged. "I have never been afraid to pursue what I desire."

"Very well, Iris," he said, a sly smile on his face that, while handsome, was also far too contrived. "I shall see you there. I eagerly await our time together."

Iris smiled and nodded before sauntering out the door. The moment the sunlight hit her face, she practically gagged. She certainly hoped Millie appreciated this — and that she captured her man, Burt. Nothing else could ever be worth it.

## 2

August Williams, the Earl of Westwood, rested his head upon his arms, which were crossed upon the desk in front of him. He stared at a glass of amber liquid from where it sat beside a half-empty bottle.

That damned bottle was currently the only thing providing him any comfort. His only friend, his only reassurance in this cruel world.

Well, perhaps he was being slightly too dramatic. He did have friends. The problem was that they all knew of his current predicament, and he had no desire to speak to any of them of it much longer.

And his best friend... well, he hadn't turned out to be much of a friend at all.

He had just reached a hand out to take another sip when there was a knock at the door.

"My lord?" his butler implored, his voice somewhat tremulous as he had, unfortunately, been the recipient of August's foul moods for more than a week now. "You have a visitor."

"I am not in residence."

*An Earl for Iris*

"You bloody well are, Westwood."

August sat up straight, sobering quickly. "General," he said, now standing at attention. "My apologies. I had no idea—"

"Sit, Westwood. Time is of the essence."

August did as he was bid by one of the few men who could evoke such ready agreement from him. General Dobbins was the very reason he had found himself involved with the Crown in the fight against the French. The man had recruited him for a very specific purpose, but as far as August was aware, his commitment was now finished and he was free to live the life he chose — though such a life had proven no longer available to him.

"What seems to be amiss, General?"

"Have you noticed anything untoward lately?" the older gentleman asked, ignoring him, as he stared at him through eyes surrounded by creases of worry, his brow furrowed. August shook his head no as he offered his superior a seat. Despite his concern, he couldn't help appreciating the General's significant mustache, which was a sight to behold.

"I'm not sure what you mean," he answered.

"Anyone following you? New acquaintances?"

"No," August said, though he didn't add that he had hardly left his townhouse since his return just over a month ago, on the night he had discovered the truth, which had changed his life forever.

"Very well," the General said, sitting back in his chair and crossing his arms over his chest. "I have some unfortunate news, Westwood. When we first brought you home from France months ago, we did so because we thought your identity had been compromised. We were loath to have you return, for you were quite well accepted within the French courts."

A role that had been rather enjoyable, for both his purpose there as an English spy as well as the lavish parties and occasions in which he had taken part.

"Yes, but I thought that you had ascertained there was nothing of which to be worried. It was the reason you had told me I could return to London following my short stay in Southwold at the flowery inn."

The General sighed. "It appears we were mistaken — the second time. Our sources tell us that your true identity emerged. The French were embarrassed by their trust in you, and few know who you really are. However, it seems they have sent someone after you, for they are unsure of what else you may know that you have not yet shared."

"I have shared all of my intelligence, General, I assure you of that," August said, wondering if perhaps the General was simply being overly cautious.

"I trust that you have," the man responded agreeably. "But I believe they are worried about information you may hold that is of an importance of which you are not even aware."

August pondered that for a moment. He supposed there could be some truth to the thought. He had become acquainted with many in the French court, and had been trusted by most. Who knows what could prove to be useful to the English one day?

"Interesting," he said, leaning back now, before belatedly offering the General a drink.

"No, thank you," said the man. "I am surprised, Westwood. You are handling this with much less concern than I would have thought. You do understand that your life could be in danger, do you not?"

"My life was in danger since I left for France," August

said, though he didn't add that now he no longer cared as much about it. For when he departed England's shores nearly a year ago, he had something — someone — to return home to. Now, the promise of her was gone, and he was alone. He had his mother and sister, sure. He loved them and knew he must provide for them. But were anything to happen to him, his brother was ready and willing to take the title of earl.

August hadn't possessed such a title when he had left England. He hadn't learned of his father's death until returning to England's shores, and he was left with a sense of guilt that he had missed his father's last days. But he knew the previous earl had been proud of him and his commitment to his country. At least he had that assurance to live with.

"We will do all we can to keep you safe," the General said now. "But we think it's best that you return to hiding."

"To hiding? No thank you, General, I will take my chances."

August had no wish to return to Southwold. It had been a beautiful place, true, but he couldn't fathom the thought of moving backward. It would also remind him of a time when he had been anticipating his return to his love, a woman who had proven to be less than faithful and certainly not as inclined to wait for him as he for her.

"Unfortunately, the choice is not yours to make," the General said, standing as if to prove that their conversation truly was over. "We cannot put the lives of our men at risk by following you around London. And we also have no desire for you to be captured and interrogated, for you may pass valuable information back to the French. No, Westwood, for the time being you will return to The Wild Rose Inn. You must leave by tomorrow."

"Tomorrow?" he echoed, aghast, belatedly rising as well. "General, I apologize, but I simply cannot. I—"

"You will be accompanied by two soldiers, who will then leave you at the inn. You will ride on horseback so that you do not draw any attention to your station nor your identity. The last thing we need is the crest of the Earl of Westwood upon a carriage riding down along England's roads. I wish you well, son. We will be in touch when you are able to return home once more."

"But what could change?" August asked desperately. "If you find my potential attacker, could not more follow?"

"They could," the General agreed. "We will find those who pursue you, and hopefully have the opportunity to determine what they know and what they plan to do with you. As I said, we will be in touch, Westwood. Safe travels."

As he departed the room, August could only stare after him before sinking back down into his chair, his head in his hands. He hadn't anticipated that his life could become any worse than it was already. Apparently, he was wrong.

## 3

Iris hummed a little tune to herself as she trimmed the tulips in the garden in front of the inn. You would think her mother would have planted roses for the inn's namesake, she thought to herself with a smile. Not that the type of flora seemed to matter, as the inn was full of furniture and patterns of every floral arrangement one could ever imagine. It was rather gaudy, that was for certain, but Iris had learned long ago that it was one subject not to broach with Alice Tavners. Her mother didn't care about much, but this was one aspect that did raise her ire.

Iris sat back on her heels, dusting the dirt off of her white muslin dress inlaid with a pattern of pink roses. She smiled ironically at herself.

Well, no one could ever accuse her of not making an effort here at the inn. Since Daisy and then Marigold had married and left not only the inn but Southwold, many of the tasks had fallen to Iris and her younger sister, Violet. Thankfully, their father had also hired a couple of additional hands around the house to assist their previous one maid, Maria.

Iris bit her lip as she looked at the flowerbed in front of her. She hadn't realized just how much she would come to miss her sisters. Oh, they had clashed more than a few times, that was for certain, but in the end, there was no one closer to her than the women she had grown up with.

She had encouraged the two of them to marry, for she thought she would then have her own prospects open up. But everything had changed when one man in particular had captured her heart.

"Miss Iris?"

The voice cut through her musings and startled Iris so much that she gave a little shriek and fell backward, over her heels and onto her bottom. She closed her eyes for but a moment as she shook her head. She recognized that voice. But no — it couldn't be. August Williams had departed the inn months ago without a backward glance. His face had been directed forward, toward the woman who was awaiting him at home in London. He couldn't be back. No, it was simply her imagination acting up.

"Are you all right?"

Suddenly there were strong hands around her waist, their warmth creeping in through the muslin of her dress, and Iris still refused to open her eyes, for then this dream would end and she would be back alone in the dirt once more.

The hands, however, swiveled her around, and soon she had no choice but to open her eyes — and look up into the warm, dark brown depths that she remembered so well, that she had tried to forget and to push from her mind so that she might move on and accept another.

"Lord Westwood," she breathed, noting the way his eyes crinkled at the corners as he smiled at her — or laughed at her, she wasn't entirely sure. Iris attempted to maintain her

*An Earl for Iris*

composure, taking deep breaths, which seemed to cause him to realize just where his hands were as her ribs expanded and contracted underneath them. He quickly dropped his arms and stepped back from her, the perfect gentleman once more.

"My apologies," he said. "I certainly did not mean to startle you."

"It's fine. You didn't," she said quickly, then amended her words. "Or, rather, you did, but it was my own fault, as I was lost in my reveries."

She affixed a smile to her face, attempting to mask the quick beating of her heart. She had convinced herself that she felt nothing for this man, that she would remember him as only a brief infatuation, a handsome stranger who had passed through the inn and who would remain nothing more than a lovely memory.

Of course, she also hadn't thought she would ever see him again, which made all the difference.

"What are you doing here?" she asked, blurting out the words, not at all the polished flirtation she had so practiced and usually perfected.

"Iris!" Her father admonished from behind her now as he had stepped out of the front entrance of the inn. "That is rather impertinent. It matters not *why* Lord Westwood is here. Come in, my lord, we may discuss this in my office."

Lord Westwood offered Iris a quick nod and a smile before following her father into the inn. Iris noted then that he had what looked to be a saddlebag in his hand. So the Earl was returning to their inn, then, for at the very least a brief stay. Whatever could he be doing here once more?

As soon as they were out of sight, Iris followed them into the inn, tiptoeing down the corridor until she reached her father's study. She knelt down, pressing her eye against the keyhole, but then silently cursed. Her father still had the hole blocked.

"Attempting to discover something?"

Iris jumped, causing her to hit her head on the doorknob.

"Ouch!" she exclaimed, rubbing the top of her head as she turned to face her younger sister, Violet. "You startled me."

"I thought you knew Father had blocked the hole from your prying eyes and ears," Violet said with a smile as she crossed her arms over her chest and contemplated her sister.

"Yes, well, I thought it was worth a try," Iris said with a sigh. "Lord Westwood has returned."

"Lord Westwood?" That bit of information even captured Violet's attention. "I thought he had returned to London."

"I thought so, too," Iris said.

Suddenly the door to their father's study opened a crack and their Father's greying head peered out.

"Girls," he admonished. "We can hear your jabbering from within. What are you doing out here?"

"Iris is attempting to listen in to your conversation, of course," Violet said with a bit of a giggle and Iris shot a glare toward her.

"I was not. I was simply passing by to see to my duties and met Violet in the corridor. We were discussing what to prepare for dinner tonight. Would the Earl like anything in particular?"

"I'm sure our dinner is the furthest thing from the Earl's mind at the moment," her father chastised them, but then a voice called out from within the room.

"I fancy roast duck, actually!"

*An Earl for Iris*

Iris' eyes widened as she and Violet shared a look before they both began to laugh. Their father's face turned bright red and then he shut the door on the two of them to return to the room and the man he was clearly trying to impress, a task at which he was failing miserably — like always.

Iris shook her head as she urged Violet down the hall.

"Well," she said, "roast duck it is, I suppose. We'd best get to the kitchens."

Iris sighed, and they continued on their way, though despite their task, her mind wouldn't leave their new arrival and her heart was reminded of what she had felt for him.

∽

AUGUST WAS RELIEVED to finally escape from Elias Tavners' study. He hadn't wanted to share his entire story with the man, but the innkeeper, clearly missing his own days on the battlefield as part of the war effort, had coaxed much of it out of him.

Tavners found the story much more intriguing than August himself, to be sure.

So here he was, once more, wandering the guest quarters of The Wild Rose Inn. Southwold was a pretty, peaceful town, but there wasn't overly much to keep oneself entertained. Sure, there had been street fairs and there was ample opportunity for walks and the like, but it was not as though there was a bustling social scene like that which he was used to — both in England and during his time in France. There was the ale house to pass the nights, but August had seen enough drunk soldiers for a lifetime.

As he walked toward the sitting room, August caught a glimpse of white fabric float around the corner. Iris Tavners. He had been surprised at the wave of pleasure that had coursed through him upon seeing her again, crouched in the garden with that look of contemplation on her face.

He had been entertained by her during his previous visit — she was a woman who knew how to find the fun in life — but he had been so preoccupied with returning home to Amelia that besides noticing, for a moment, Iris' beauty as any man would, he hadn't thought much more about her.

Of course, there had been that moment of misunderstanding, when she must have thought he was leaning in to take her lips, but he had quickly cleared that up. He hoped it wouldn't be an issue anymore, for he was clearly going to be here for some time.

"Lord Westwood?"

He looked up at the door of the sitting room, realizing now that he was standing like a fool in the midst of the floral walls and furniture, staring at everything and nothing at the same time.

"Miss Violet," he greeted the youngest daughter. She looked like her sister, but was willowy, pixie-like with lighter hair, whereas Iris was striking. "How do you do?"

"Very well, my lord," she said with a gentle smile. "I know you have spoken with my father, but as always, if there is anything you need upon your stay, please feel free to ask any of us. We do have a few other guests at the moment. I believe they are currently out fishing."

Fishing. August managed a smile for the girl, but it was somewhat forced. He couldn't remember the last time he had fished. He must have been a boy.

"Thank you, Miss Violet," he said, and she nodded and turned to leave before pausing for a moment at the door.

"Oh, and tomorrow night there is to be a dance at the Johnsons' farm. You are invited, of course, as are the rest of our guests. We do hope you will join us."

August nodded. He truly had no wish to attend a dance. It would remind him of the last dance he'd attended, when he had to stand and watch his former fiancée and his best friend, now husband and wife, take to the floor. The evening had not ended well — he'd had far too many drinks and had caused quite a scene before his brother had escorted him out of Almack's. He cringed as he recalled the humiliation. It had been the last social event he had attended before he had sworn them all off. Once the man who had been at the center of many social engagements, after that he became something of a recluse, besides the odd visit to a club or two.

For he no longer trusted women — any woman. He had thought Amelia was one who would love him and wait for him no matter what, but her affections had proven fickle. While he was serving his country, she had found comfort in the arms of another.

At least no one here knew of all that had transpired in London. He *would* go to this dance, charm a few of the local young women, and continue on as he had been — waiting for the day he would be told that he was no longer in any danger and could return to his former life. What that life would hold, he had no idea. But it was what he knew and he didn't see any other options left.

## 4

Iris tried to convince herself that the only reason she was taking extra care with her appearance tonight was due to the fact that she was supposed to be attracting the attention of Ernest Abernathy. It absolutely was not because of a certain Lord Westwood — the man was out of her reach for more reasons than she could count on one hand.

And yet, when she walked down the stairs of the family side of the inn, she couldn't help the rapid beating of her heart, nor keep her eyes from wandering to the door of the guest quarters where she knew he would be waiting.

Damn him. Why did he have to return? And damn her own fickle heart. She could have any matter of young men from the village and yet here she was, unable to keep her thoughts from Lord Westwood. Well, she might have no control over her *thoughts*, but she could certainly control her actions. She determined that she would spend the entirety of the night as well as the remainder of his stay here ignoring him as much as possible.

"Well, aren't my daughters looking lovely tonight?" Her

mother exclaimed as Iris reached the bottom step. Violet had been ready ages ago, but Iris had always taken much longer to prepare herself. Tonight she wore a pretty lavender dress which hugged her generous curves and highlighted the deep chestnut of her hair and her crystal-blue eyes.

"Are we finally ready?" Her father's voice boomed as he entered the room. "The carriage awaits."

The boarders who chose to attend apparently would meet them there, having decided to ride their own horses. Iris attempted to temper down her disappointment at the thought as Violet sent a knowing, pitying look her way — one Iris chose to ignore.

The carriage ride was short, and Iris almost convinced herself that tonight was going to be fun and entertaining — most people from the village and the surrounding area would be in attendance, and it was a night for celebration. The Johnson farm had burned to the ground many months ago, and the family had become particularly close with the Tavnerses as they had stayed at the inn during the rebuilding. The village had come together for them, and tonight they would all celebrate the friendship and renewal of their home.

And then Iris disembarked from the carriage, and her mood immediately dove. For there awaiting her was Ernest Abernathy. Drat it all. Oh, how she wished she had never made this promise to Millie. She saw Violet look from the intent Ernest back to her, and soon her sister was in her ear.

"What is happening between you and Ernest Abernathy?" Violet whispered, and Iris shook her head.

"Nothing," she hissed. "Nothing at all."

"Then why is he standing there grinning at you like a fool?"

Iris sighed, turning to Violet now so that Ernest hopefully wouldn't know what they were saying.

"It's a long story, but I'm doing a favor for Millie."

"*You* are?"

Iris narrowed her eyes at her sister.

"Is that so difficult to believe?"

"Well," Violet said, nibbling her bottom lip, her eyes, the color of her name, studying Iris. "I wouldn't say it is a particularly frequent occurrence."

"As it happens, I have a romantic heart myself, Vi," she said. "And I wish for Millie to live a life of love. In order for that to happen, she needs to rid herself of Ernest. And that's where I come in."

"Oh dear," was all Violet said as Ernest approached. He lifted Iris' hand and bent low over it as though they were a lord and lady greeting one another at a ball.

"Iris Tavners, you look as lovely as ever," he said, his eyes raking over her in a way that caused Iris to feel as though he had invaded her very personal space. "I am so complimented that you have made an extra effort tonight for me."

Behind his back, Violet made a noise that sounded as though she were choking, and it was all Iris could do to not join in.

She wished now that she hadn't tried so hard, for it was not for Ernest, but someone else entirely.

As Ernest began to rise from his bent position over her hand, her gaze caught a profile beyond.

A group of riders was cresting the hill, though there was one in particular she focused on. He was hard to miss. She didn't think she had ever seen shoulders so broad nor a man who held himself with such confidence. She knew the moment he saw her as well, for his horse slowed and despite the setting sun, she could have sworn he stared at her for

*An Earl for Iris*

just a moment, but then he nudged his horse and was off toward the barn once more.

Not that it mattered, she told herself. He was taken by another, and she was moving on. Though not, she told herself as she looked in front of her, with Ernest Abernathy.

"Perhaps we should reconvene later on for our dance?" she asked him now, attempting a pretty smile.

"I was hoping to escort you inside, Miss Iris," he said. "You are the most beautiful woman in attendance tonight, I am sure. We will look quite fine walking in together."

Goodness, the man was arrogant. Iris opened her mouth to tell him exactly what she thought of his statement, but then she saw Millie arriving with her father, the local blacksmith. She was looking one way and then the other, and Iris was well aware of who she sought out the moment her eyes settled upon someone in the distance, a large smile crossing her face.

One night, Iris, she told herself. You can do this. She glanced over at Violet, who gave her a nod of encouragement. Even her sister was proud of her for doing what was hopefully the right thing. Iris squared her shoulders, steeled her resolve, and took Ernest's arm, though she kept her body as far from him as she possibly could.

～

AUGUST HAD BEEN to many social gatherings throughout his lifetime, but none that were anything like this. He had attended balls at Almack's, parties at some of the most opulent houses in London, and gatherings at grand estates throughout the countryside.

They had been attended by dukes and duchesses,

nobility of every tier, and once even the Prince Regent himself had been at the same event.

None of it had prepared him for a country dance in a new barn.

As he stepped inside, he was overwhelmed by the fresh smell of the newly hewn timber and brick, and the sweet smell of the hay sitting in the corner awaiting distribution following tonight's festivities.

August didn't think he had ever actually been in a true barn before. Stables, of course, but a barn for animals? He didn't think so.

There was a low hum resounding around the barn as people began to gather within, greeting one another with smiles, embraces, and handshakes. August stood by the door with the few other men he had arrived with. They were outsiders in this event which was for the locals. He shouldn't have come. None of them should have. Then, the din was overwhelmed by the startup of instruments that until now had been sitting in the corner of the barn. A trio of men now held them and began playing a lively tune. People of all ages took to the floor, swinging one another around in a dance that was as uncoordinated as it was spirited. August found himself tapping his foot in time to the music, his feet itching to join in on the dance floor.

He was soon distracted, however, by a vision in purple who walked through the door. Certainly, he wasn't the only one whose attention was captured by the woman. He'd thought he had seen Iris Tavners in the distance when he arrived. But now, seeing her so close, as beautiful as she ever was, she actually took his breath away.

Her chestnut curls were pulled back in a simple yet elegant style that framed her face, and he was taken aback by his urgent need to have his arms about her waist. He was

*An Earl for Iris*

perplexed. Where was this coming from? How many times had he seen her in the past when he previously boarded at The Wild Rose Inn? True, was he being honest with himself, he had been unable to resist the attraction that he felt for her, despite the fact he had the woman he'd once thought loved him waiting for him at home.

Just then, he noted something else — Iris was not alone. Her hand rested on the arm of another man. A man with perfectly coiffed blond hair, who would likely be considered as good looking as she. August didn't think he had ever seen the man before, and he couldn't remember Iris being attached to anyone. Sure, he knew she was a woman who was popular with the young men in the area, and he had always been aware that she was something of a flirt. She certainly had been with him and he assumed she was with most young men she encountered.

August noted the pride in the man's gaze as he looked around the room, clearly appreciating the fact that the two of them were being noticed by most. He led her onto the dance floor, and August wondered if it was his imagination, or if Iris seemed reluctant to join her partner. Either way, August soon had to tear his gaze away, or else he was sure that others would notice the attention he was paying to the two of them.

Which was why, an hour later, he was surprised when Iris approached him. August had taken a couple of turns on the dance floor himself but was now enjoying a drink with some of the other men from the inn. Most had been fighting in the war, though no one revealed much about themselves. Still, they were companions with a similar past and shared a common understanding among them.

"Lord Westwood," Iris said, approaching him, he

stepped away from the other men. "Are you enjoying yourself this evening?"

"I am," he said. "Though clearly not as much as you are."

She looked at him with some confusion, likely due to the sarcasm that had unwittingly entered his tone.

"I am having a fine enough time," she said.

"I was unaware that you were attached," August said, trying to adopt an air of nonchalance — one that he should be holding regardless. In fact, he had no idea why he was even questioning her about this. It was certainly none of his business and would not affect him or his life.

"Oh, *I* am *not* attached," she said, causing him to raise an eyebrow.

"Truly?" he asked. "Conventions must be considerably different here in Southwold. Where I am from if a lady arrived with a gentleman and then danced more than twice with him one would consider her spoken for."

"I can assure you that is not the case," she said, but as though to disprove her words she was joined by the man to whom he had been referring.

"Iris, darling," he said, "please introduce me to this man."

A dark look flitted across her face for a moment before she reestablished her winning smile.

"Lord Westwood, may I please introduce Ernest Abernathy? Mr. Abernathy, this is Lord August Williams, one of the guests at our inn."

"It is a pleasure," August murmured, but he certainly didn't mean the words when he saw the way the man glared at him with a silent warning to stay away.

Well, this was interesting. Iris was obviously lying about her relationship. Should he even be surprised? After all that had occurred with Amelia, he should know better. Iris was obviously just another woman keeping her options open, despite the fact that she was already promised to one man.

"Shall we rejoin the dance floor?" her Mr. Abernathy asked, nearly ignoring August altogether.

"Actually," she said, "Lord Westwood just asked if I would accompany him for a set." She looked at August now, her eyes pleading. "I told him I would be happy to, isn't that right, Lord Westwood?"

He should tell this poor fellow here the truth of the matter, but he was too curious for his own good. He wanted to know what the woman was up to. What that said about his own life and his lack of stimulation, he wasn't entirely sure, but how much harm could one dance do?

## 5

"Thank you," Iris breathed as the two of them joined the other couples on the dance floor, where the music and therefore the movement of the people had slowed to a gentle sway.

"To what are you referring?"

"For agreeing to this dance despite the fact you never actually asked me."

"You didn't want another dance with your *darling* Mr. Abernathy?" Lord Westwood asked, and she cringed at his words as he took one of her hands in his and placed the other upon her waist. She tried not to react to his touch, though it was difficult to ignore the tremors that ran down her spine — far from the chill she had felt when Earnest placed his hands upon her.

"He's *not* my darling," she said. "Far from it, in fact. It's a long story, but all I must do is put up with him for a short time."

"Until when?" he asked, his face displaying his confusion.

Iris opened her mouth to respond, but just then she saw

Millie's father pass behind Lord Westwood. "I will explain another time," she promised.

August nodded, but Iris didn't miss the dark look that crossed his face and she wondered at it. Why did he care?

She was about to ask him what had caused such a reaction when she noticed something — rather, someone — else across the room.

"Oh, dear," she murmured, already attempting to determine just how she could resolve the situation when Lord Westwood cut into her thoughts.

"What is it?"

"My sister," she said with a sigh. "Violet. There she is, standing in the corner as always. I do wish she would try a little harder. Once we are finished our dance I shall find a nice gentleman to join her. From there, hopefully she will realize just how much fun dancing can be and will join in the festivities."

A half-smile had grown on Lord Westwood's face.

"And what if she does not want to dance?" he asked.

"Of course she wants to dance," Iris said, rolling her eyes at him. "Who wouldn't? She simply will not be encouraging anyone to ask her if she continues to stand there as she is."

Lord Westwood shrugged. "Some people would rather remain in the shadows. Although I suppose a woman like you might not completely understand that."

Iris bristled. "Forgive me, but what exactly does that mean?"

Lord Westwood chuckled at her indignation, which only further fueled it.

"Only that everyone is different, Miss Iris. You enjoy interaction with other people, while your sister obviously does not."

"Which is why she requires a bit of help now and then,"

Iris said pointedly, and Lord Westwood just sighed, giving up on his attempt to convince her otherwise, and rightly so. He didn't know her sister as she did.

"Anyway," Iris said airily in an attempt to keep him from realizing how his apparent disdain for her actions affected her, "tell me, Lord Westwood, after your last stay, did you return to London and wed the love of your life?"

She was tossing his own words back at him. She had tried to push away the memory of their last encounter, but she couldn't help the way it continued to repeat itself over and over in her mind.

She had run into him in the corner outside of the guest sitting room. The bedding she had been carrying had fallen to the floor and they both bent to pick it up at the same time. Their heads had bumped into one another ever so slightly, and when she looked up, his lips were but a breath away from hers. When their eyes met, she had thought what she saw in them was what she was feeling deep inside herself — a longing desire. Iris had leaned in, but when she did he pulled back abruptly, leaving her bereft and embarrassed.

He had apologized, blaming himself for the misunderstanding, and then went on to explain that he would be returning to London and about the woman he would soon marry — the love of his life. They would have already been wed, he told her, had her father not been away in Scotland until after Lord Westwood left to work for the Crown.

Now, in response to Iris' question, he went completely still, stopping all movements of the dance. His eyes flashed dark, his expression one she could only describe as haunted.

"She was not, apparently, the love of my life," he said, his voice devoid of all emotion. "At the very least, I was not hers."

*An Earl for Iris*

"Oh," Iris said, unsure of how to respond to his words. She was shocked and longed to know more of what had happened, but she had no idea how to ask without causing him to completely shut down. "I-I'm sorry to hear it."

"Yes, well, so was I," he said, only now beginning to move once more after they had been bumped into by other couples on the floor. "But there is nothing to be done now."

Should she ask what had occurred? If the woman was well? Iris bit her lip but just then the music came to a stop and bloody Ernest was there once more at her elbow, waiting for the next dance.

"I will leave you to your gentleman," Lord Westwood said, and as he began to walk away, Iris brushed aside Ernest's waiting arms.

"I need some refreshment," she grumbled, no longer caring, for the moment at least, how she might appear to him.

He opened his mouth to argue with her but must have seen how disgruntled she was and promptly shut it. Iris mused that perhaps he had finally smartened some, but then he followed along behind her.

"Did Lord Westerland say something to offend you?" he asked.

"Lord Westwood," Iris muttered. "And no, he didn't."

"Did he—"

"Ernest, could you please just shov—"

"Iris!"

Iris hadn't realized she had walked right into Millie, who was walking toward the dance floor behind Burt. "So lovely to see you," Millie continued, a smile on her face as she looked between Iris and Ernest.

"And you, Millie," Iris said, her face flooding with heat at what Millie had likely overheard. Once again, Iris was allowing her own interests and emotions to overcome all else. "You look well this evening."

"As do you."

They shared a look of understanding, and Iris swallowed the words she had been about to spew forth to her companion.

"I shall leave you. Come, Ernest," she sighed. "Let's find a drink."

And put all thought of Lord Westwood and his former fiancée behind her. For there was one thing Iris refused to be — and that was anyone's second choice.

~

August wiped his brow as he exited the dance floor. The night was coming to a close, and the villagers began to trickle out of the building. He had danced a few sets with some of the pretty local women, but he couldn't help that one dance of the night that had stood out in his mind. One with a young woman who was far too willful, far too obstinate, and far too inquisitive. One thing was for certain — it was difficult to know what to expect when it came to Iris Tavners.

He didn't know why he had revealed so much to her when she had asked about Amelia. He would have preferred to leave his life in London where it was — in London. If there was one benefit to returning to Southwold, it was that here, no one knew of the circumstances regarding his broken engagement nor his humiliation.

At the very least, the dance had ended before she had the opportunity to question him any further. Her beau had arrived, ready to sweep her back onto the dance floor. Why she had been particularly rude to Abernarthy, he had no

*An Earl for Iris*

idea. It was almost as though she were attempting to be rid of him. But if there was one thing he had learned upon his last visit, the girl was not short of suitors. So why would she simply not tell him to shove off and leave her be? It was perplexing, though, he told himself, not at all his problem to concern himself over.

What had truly caused him the most worry, however, was not her inability to understand her sister, nor the man she tossed aside when she had the opportunity to dance with an earl, nor even the fact she had questioned him far more than he desired regarding his love life — or lack thereof. No, what was truly bothering him, what he did not want to accept, was what she had stirred within him. For when her warm yet delicate fingers had been encased in his, when he had placed his hand upon her waist just where it began to flare out into a voluptuous hip, desire had flickered to life deep within him and had fanned out throughout his extremities.

Her crystal-blue eyes had seemingly pierced right through him when she looked at him, and when she stepped closer, a scent that seemed to be a mixture of lavender and lemon had wafted up from her hair to his nose, and he had to restrain himself from leaning down for more.

No, he thought, following his fellow soldiers as they rode down the hill from the barn and back to the village, time spent with Iris Tavners was nothing but dangerous. She was not a woman to trust — though how many of them were? And worse still, it was his own fickle emotions that most worried him. He had proven to be a terrible judge of character in the past, and no pretty face was going to cause him such heartache again. Of that, he was sure.

## 6

Iris stared at the task in front of her and began to slowly back out the door, only to bump into Violet behind her, who was continuing down the corridor to the next bedchamber.

"No you don't," Violet said, clicking her tongue. "The sooner you begin, the sooner it will be done."

Iris closed her eyes for a moment, hoping that the disheveled bedchamber would disappear by the time she opened them once more. Unfortunately no miracle occurred and the disheveled bedroom remained.

Another boarder had left and a new one would soon be arriving — meaning that by this afternoon the room had to be in a state to welcome someone new.

"Perhaps this is a task best left to one of the new maids," she said, chewing her lip.

"Then you should get to the kitchens and take over peeling potatoes," Violet said over her shoulder as she continued on, and Iris sighed and stepped into the room with her bucket of water and a rag.

Iris was becoming rather tired of this work. She was not

*An Earl for Iris*

meant to act as a servant within an inn. Her sister Daisy had been much more suited to this. She had never complained and, in fact, seemed to relish the opportunity to take care of others. Then she had married a duke and now she had legions of servants doing everything for her. It was hardly fair.

But that was life, was it not? Iris steeled her shoulders and entered the room, bristling at the mess. This guest hadn't been particularly clean, unfortunately. She crossed to the other wall, opening a window to allow the sea breeze to waft in and begin to air out the room. She stood there for a moment, enjoying the view of the waves gently lapping the shore. It was beautiful here, that she certainly couldn't deny. She sighed before turning and set to work, determined not to allow the chore to dim her spirits. She began to hum as she went about her work until the melody eventually took over and the words began to flow, the song as natural to her as breathing itself.

~

AUGUST WAS RETURNING to his room after the morning walk he had decided would become a habit during his stay at Southwold. Well, the habit so far had been consistent for two days, but his plan was for it to continue. He had to admit that the ocean air was refreshing and to be out of the bustle of London was soothing for the soul.

It was interesting, for August had always enjoyed being surrounded by people, whether it be at his gentlemen's club or at a social gathering of one sort or the other. Whether he was conversing with other men or flirting with women, he had never found it overly difficult to attract people to him or to encourage conversation.

Here in Southwold, he found himself alone more often and yet when he was within the village or around others of the town, there was a certain familiarity, despite the fact that he was a stranger. No one put on airs or cared whether he had recently lunched with a duke or had a tryst with lady so-and-so. When the man serving him a drink asked him if he was having an enjoyable evening, he knew the man actually cared about whether or not he had. It was as refreshing as the ocean air itself.

As he continued down the corridor, a nearby sound stopped him right where he stood. It was coming from within one of the chambers, and so out of place he couldn't help his surprise. But it wasn't anything concerning, rather... it was a melody, a song, a siren's call, he thought as he drew closer. While he wasn't a man who could profess to create music himself, he certainly appreciated it as much as any person did. But this was different. For no matter whether or not it was appropriate to do so, he found himself inching ever closer to the door, his hand coming to the handle, turning the knob to peek inside to determine what — or who — could be creating such beauty.

He stood there for a moment, transfixed at the sight in front of him. A linen gown covered her frame, yet still August was more than aware of the curves beneath it. Her hair was loosely tied back away from her face, a kerchief covering many of the curls, yet still, some escaped and cascaded down her back. Her hands grasped the corners of a blanket that she crisply cracked through the air before she settled it down on the bed beneath. As she went about her tasks, her voice never broke as the words and the tune flowed from her as though it was a part of her.

August wasn't sure how long he stood there. It was only when he shifted his weight and the floorboard beneath him cracked that Iris spun around to face him, halting her melody.

"My apologies," he said quickly. "I had no wish to disturb you. I heard your song and wondered, I suppose, how a soldier could make such beautiful music."

He laughed, hoping his embarrassment would help her forget the fact he had been so openly admiring her.

"Of course," he continued, "I should have known it was you after hearing you sing with your sisters the last time I stayed here at the inn."

"Oh," she said, waving her hand in the air, "I had nearly forgotten about that. I appreciate the compliment, but really, it's all just for a bit of fun."

"I'm not so sure about that," he said in all honesty. "I've seen some of the most famous women in the world sing on stage and you could be up there with them."

"Stop," she said, her cheeks turning pink, but he could tell she appreciated his words. "I am nothing of the sort. I mostly sing for my own amusement."

"Though your sisters didn't seem to enjoy themselves when you hosted the musicale."

"No," she said, biting her lip in a way that was rather endearing. "I always thought perhaps if they could hear us together they could see that we should sing or perform more often, but... they never found as much enjoyment in it as I did. They all have beautiful voices, however, and I just wish they would showcase them."

He shrugged, leaning against the doorframe. "Not everyone enjoys being on display."

"Fair point," she said, returning to her work, folding blankets and placing them on a nearby chair. "And you, Lord Westwood? You strike me as the kind of man who enjoys himself around others."

"I do," he agreed. "Or, rather, I did. I've found myself something of a recluse as of late."

"Oh?" she said, feigning disinterest, although the woman's intentions were easy enough to see through. "Did that change recently?"

"It did."

"Did it have anything to do with your former fiancée?" She turned to him now, her face inquisitive. "That is not why you returned to the inn, was it? To distance yourself from her?"

"No," he shook his head. "I do not run from my problems. Unless I'm ordered to, that is."

"But you apparently hide from them."

She raised an eyebrow and glanced over at him pointedly, and he emitted a low chuckle.

"You are rather direct, aren't you?"

"I am," she nodded. "My father would tell you that is a great fault of mine, and he would likely be correct. I find, however, that it is often best to ask exactly what you would like to know, rather than guess or hear half-truths from others."

"That is a fair point, Miss Iris, and perhaps we would all be better off if more people thought the same."

"We would. There would be less gossip and idle chatter, *that* I can tell you."

He smiled, one of his first true smiles in some time. He liked talking to Iris Tavners, and for more reasons than simply her beautiful face.

Not that he would allow emotions to go any further than that. She may be pretty, but she wouldn't be taking over any of his actual regard.

"Well, I'm finished here," she said, walking toward him, and he was overcome once more by the smell of lavender

*An Earl for Iris*

and lemon. Where was it coming from? She must bathe in it, he thought, desire tugging at him.

"I'll help you," he said, reaching his arms out to take the bundle from her.

"Oh, don't be silly," she said, twisting so that he couldn't reach her. "If my father saw a guest — an earl no less — carrying soiled linens he would have a fit."

"That sounds entertaining," August answered with a grin, and Iris laughed. She had a loud, long laugh, one that reached into a person's soul and caused joy for the sake of joy.

"You might think. But once he gets going, well... I do not entirely enjoy being on the receiving end of such a thing."

"I see," August said, though he didn't entirely. His father had always been rather benevolent — too much so, perhaps, according to many of his peers. It may have been what led to August's ability to not overly worry about his responsibilities but rather enjoy life as it came. "You say there are more boarders arriving?" he asked, changing the subject.

"Apparently. Father never tells us much. I suspect it is because he forgets who is arriving and when," she said, rolling her eyes as August followed her through the hall and then down the staircase. "You never did tell me what brought you back here."

"Orders," he said, shrugging, preferring that she think of him as a soldier than a spy who hardly did more than enjoy himself at parties. "I did some... clandestine work. Apparently the French know more about me than they were ever supposed to."

"Really?" she asked, a spark coming to her eye as she turned and looked at him. "Now *that* sounds rather intriguing."

"I suppose some of it is," he said. "Other parts of it are not."

She stopped on the stairs now and narrowed her eyes at him. "Are you in danger?"

He wasn't sure how to answer that.

"I doubt it," he finally said. "But there was a chance that my identity had been compromised, and so I returned here for a time. Just to be safe."

She tilted her head to the side, contemplating his words. "You do not think that there is any danger to the rest of us here at the inn — do you?"

He would be lying if he didn't admit that the thought had briefly crossed his mind. Wherever he went, if what the General told him was true, he could be putting others in jeopardy. But this was where he had been ordered to go, and this was where he would stay until he heard otherwise.

"You will be fine," he said with what he hoped was a reassuring smile before they parted ways at the bottom of the stairs. "I'll make sure of it."

7

"Violet?"

Iris had no idea where her sister was. She had looked everywhere around the inn trying to find her. They had to start preparing the evening meal for the boarders, and Iris was certainly not doing it alone. It was not like Violet to disappear. Sure, there was the odd time she would lose track of time with her head stuck in one book or another, but Iris had checked all of her usual haunts and couldn't find her anywhere.

Iris was crossing by the front foyer when she heard a voice — a man's and... Violet's. Was Violet laughing? Flirting? No, certainly not. It couldn't be. Iris tiptoed to the open door, standing beside it to better listen to the conversation within.

"Had I known The Wild Rose Inn held such a beautiful young woman, perhaps I would have traveled here faster," the man said, and when Violet giggled — giggled! — Iris peered around the corner to get a better look.

The man was certainly good looking, though perhaps not in the traditional sense. He was tall, rather lean, and held himself with an arrogant swagger that Iris knew all too well — she had seen it in Ernest far too often recently. This man's hair was so blond it nearly shone white, and his eyes... oh dear. They were now trained on her. He had caught her spying. But instead of calling out to her or saying anything regarding her stare, he simply returned to complimenting Violet. Well, this was interesting. Iris took a step into the foyer.

"Violet, is this one of our new guests?" she asked, and when Violet turned to her, her cheeks were flushed a bright pink, her eyes sparkling.

"It is," she said. "Iris, please meet Thomas Cooper. Mr. Cooper, my sister, Iris."

"A pleasure," he said before returning to Violet. "Miss Violet, would you show me to my room?"

"Of course," Violet said, deliberately not meeting Iris' gaze as she turned to walk by her to the stairs. "Right this way."

As he walked after Violet, Thomas Cooper turned and finally looked at Iris — only his gaze didn't seem so friendly anymore. They locked eyes for a moment, and when they did, an eerie chill ran down Iris' spine.

She knew if she told anyone they would tell her she was being distrustful, that she was assuming far too much from one look. But Iris could read people. And something about this man told her that he was one she must keep her eye on.

～

AUGUST ENTERED the dining room to find that the two seats which had been left empty by the departing boarders were filled once again. One man was rather nondescript, who said nothing of note besides a quick hello, introducing

*An Earl for Iris*

himself as Mr. Ridlington, but the other enthusiastically greeted him when he entered.

"Lord Westwood," he said, as August perused his white-blond hair and lanky build. "I have heard much about you. I am very pleased to meet you."

August nodded at him, curious. "In what regard do you know of me?"

"Why, by your exploits of course," the man said, winking at him, and August raised an eyebrow.

"How very interesting," he said. "As far as I was aware, my actions were known to very few."

"I have my ways," the man said with a friendly smile, and August wondered just who he was and what his role had been within the fight against Napoleon and the French. He would have to ask when there were far fewer ears about.

Dinner was fairly uneventful, though August found himself unable to tear his eyes away from Iris the few times she came in to serve. She was beautiful, true — that he had noticed since the first time he had met her. But what he had been remiss in noticing before was the air about her that drew others to her, a quality that made her difficult to resist. It left him longing to spend more time with her, to come to know her better — which was not at all ideal.

"I can see why you are attracted to her," came a voice from his right, and August turned to meet Thomas Cooper's knowing gaze. "She is a beauty. But..." he leaned in conspiratorially as though sharing a secret, "I have to admit it's the sister that I prefer."

August sat back in his chair and glanced over to Violet. She was certainly a pretty thing in her own right, but perhaps too meek for him. He had always been attracted to women with some backbone. Hence his obsession with Amelia, a temptress that every man he knew had been attracted to. He had thought himself rather lucky to win her over, but as it turned out, he had simply been the man of the moment and not hers forever.

Perhaps he should shift his interest to a woman like Violet, who was more likely to follow her future husband wherever he wished to go — and who would fulfill her promise to wait.

"Did you not just arrive?" he asked Thomas, who shrugged.

"Our first conversation was enough to convince me that she would be my ideal woman," he said. "Sometimes you know right away."

"Perhaps," he said noncommittally as he took a sip from the goblet in front of him.

"Tell me more of Southwold and of this family," Cooper said, and August looked up at him with a bit of surprise.

"I'm not sure I know much more than anyone else who has recently arrived here," he said. No one, besides the Tavners themselves, would likely be aware that he had previously stayed here. All of the boarders had changed since then.

"You seem to be friendly with them," Cooper said. "I've hardly seen the owner, as it is."

"Elias Tavners," August said, nodding his head. "He is certainly an… interesting man. His daughters basically run the inn, from what I can tell. A former soldier himself, he loves to hear of the war days. If you have any stories, I'm sure he'd love to hear them." He looked at Cooper. "What *are* your stories? Where did you fight?"

"Everywhere," Cooper said with a wink, "and nowhere. Something akin to your own work, I would venture to say."

August wasn't sure what to make of the man and his non-direct responses. Was he a spy like August? Would they

*An Earl for Iris*

have not then previously known of one another? Although most of them worked under aliases, so there was a chance that he could have not heard of the man before. Cooper, however, certainly seemed to know much about him.

"Fair enough," August finally said, taking another sip of his drink, "fair enough."

∼

IF IRIS COULD, she would slap herself.

After all that she had promised herself — to keep her emotions at bay when it came to August Williams, to not lose her head, to never, ever be a second choice — here she was, longing for him once more.

Every time they were within the same room, she seemed to be enveloped in heat from his very presence. It was ridiculous. She was a grown woman, who had spent plenty of time with other gentlemen. And yet she couldn't seem to handle a few words spoken with the man.

She had been taken off guard when he had come upon her in the guest chamber earlier that day, but she had to admit that she had enjoyed their conversation far more than she would ever want to. For now, it was more than just his rugged good looks and masculinity that was drawing her to him. It was his entire personality, one that was magnetic. She could picture him surrounded by women in London at *ton* events, the charming, good-looking earl. A hard ball of jealousy began to swirl within her stomach as she thought of it, in addition to the woman who had captured and broken his heart. What had the lady been thinking? What other man could be more enticing than him?

Not that it had anything to do with her, Iris reminded herself, as she sat at the family dining table across from her sister, with her mother and father at each end. The table seemed much larger than it ever had, and rather lonely without Daisy and Marigold. They both visited often, but it certainly wasn't the same.

"Girls," her father said, and she and Violet turned toward him. Iris knew that voice. It was the one he used when he had a suggestion for them — a suggestion that, in truth, was more so orders than anything else. "We have a fair number of guests staying with us now. Guests who are used to more entertainment than walks along the shore and night after night sitting in a small ale house."

"Isn't that why they are here, Father?" Violet asked somewhat timidly. "To find solace in what the seaside has to offer?"

He snorted. "They are here because they have been told to be here," he said, causing Violet to turn her incredulous gaze to Iris, who shrugged in response. "At any rate," he continued. "I believe we should hold an event to lift their spirits once more."

"Oh, Father," Violet cried, desperation within her voice. "Not another musicale. I cannot. Not again. Especially without Marigold here."

He turned his gaze toward her.

"I still do not know why you and Marigold were so averse to the musicale. I thought it went over quite well. However, I believe two of you is not quite enough to hold it once more. No, I think instead that we should have a sporting event of a sort. These men are used to action. We can have a tournament, and invite others from the village to partake as well."

Iris looked over to Violet, who was backing up slightly.

"I am not sure..." Violet said, shaking her head, but Iris nodded enthusiastically.

*An Earl for Iris*

"I think that is a splendid idea!" she exclaimed, which was true. She was always up for something different — something more than simply cleaning the inn and preparing meals, which was becoming rather tedious. She hadn't had nearly as much to do when Daisy and Marigold were here, but everything had changed with them gone. Now, even with the additional help, much more fell on her shoulders as well as Violet's. "What are you thinking, Father?"

"How about a tournament of different events?" her mother exclaimed from the other end of the table, clapping her hands together at the thought. "Oh, it would be such fun to watch. Iris, would you organize it?"

"When were you thinking?" she asked.

"In a week's time?" her mother questioned, and Violet was already shaking her head.

"That is so soon!" she exclaimed, but Iris waved her hand in the air.

"It will be fine. I'll ask Millie to help. "

"Oh, Iris, you were never much of a planner," Violet said with a worried frown.

"No, but I make up for it with spirit," Iris said with a grin, and Violet rolled her eyes. "It will be more fun than you could ever imagine, Violet, I promise you that."

Violet sighed, but Iris hardly noticed — she was far too busy already imagining all that was to come.

## 8

"Millie?"

Iris entered the blacksmith shop, pausing a moment to allow her eyes to adjust to the dim light within, not seeing the blacksmith as she looked about her. Millie spent much of her day within the shop or her house, helping her father, and Iris had no idea how she did so day after day. Then again, Iris often questioned how she could spend each day cleaning and cooking, but it wasn't as though she had much of a choice either.

"Iris!" Millie came out of the corner of the shop, the smile on her face only visible once she neared. "How are you? Oh, I have not properly thanked you for attracting Ernest's attention once more."

"Err... yes, well..." Iris began, knowing she had been rather remiss in the past couple of days in her mock flirtation. Ernest had come to call twice, and each time she had managed to put him off with excuses of one chore or another, but already he was becoming more insistent. "How is all developing with Burt? Do you have any idea of what might come next?"

*An Earl for Iris*

"Actually," Millie said, looking one way and then the other before taking Iris' hand in hers, "Let's step outside for a moment."

Iris nearly exclaimed, *"Thank goodness,"* but she managed to keep her thoughts within.

"What news do you have to share?" she asked once they were away from the shop and strolling down the road. Millie stopped and turned to toward Iris, taking both of her hands within hers.

"You know Burt asked me to marry him," she said, and Iris nodded. "Well, as you know, Burt is originally from Lowestoft. He had told his parents he would be asking for me, and they informed their parish, and the banns have already been read. I joined their parish so that they wouldn't be read here in Southwold."

"Oh my," Iris exclaimed, focusing on Millie's problem, though she was feeling equally as guilty about the continued charade with Ernest. "You must be thrilled!"

"I am," Millie said, but then she sobered for a moment. "Except that my father is still not pleased. I had thought if I no longer had Ernest's affections that he would accept the offer from Burt. However, he continues to turn Burt away. He told him that he was sorry but his daughter could never be the wife of a fisherman, barely getting by. What am I to do, Iris?"

Iris pressed her lips together, unsure exactly of what to say.

"I may not be the best person to ask," she began, speaking slowly. "For I can only tell you what I would do, and as many would tell you, my actions are not always what one would call overly rational."

"Tell me anyway?" Millie said, her voice and eyes pleading with Iris, who sighed.

"Very well," Iris said. "I think that you must follow your heart. If you decide that you love Burt enough that days in poverty are acceptable, then you must marry him. If you cannot accept that... then you do not. But either way, in my view, the decision is yours."

"I know," Millie responded, her voice just above a whisper, "but I do love my father."

"And if he loves you the way I know he does, then he will accept your marriage in time," Iris said as gently as she could. "But it's a risk. And risks are not meant for all of us."

"I agree," Millie said. "And normally I would not be one to make that leap. But for this... for this I am. But how do I even arrange such a marriage?"

"When is it to take place?"

"Sunday, in Lowestoft. It will take about four hours on horseback."

"Well," Iris said, a smile beginning to spread across her face. "I actually have an idea. All you must do is be prepared."

***

When August heard of this tournament of sorts, he had been both wary as well as excited for the day to arrive. He had participated in such events at house parties, of course, but he had a feeling that, like everything else he had encountered so far, this was going to be much different here in the country with regular folks.

He had to admit that he rather enjoyed the lack of pretense — perhaps he was becoming altogether too used to it, which was unfortunate, for at some point he would be returning to his true life.

Iris had been rather busy the past couple of days. When

he had caught her eye one evening after dinner and asked where she had been, she had told him that she was planning the tournament her father had announced to them all.

"You are not hiding from me, then?" he had asked with a wink, and she had blushed but had shaken her head with a smile.

"Of course not."

He was only seeking her presence out because she was the most entertaining of the lot of people who lived here, he told himself, and he would be perfectly able to quell thoughts of anything more than a friendship with her, were they to arise once more.

This morning, he joined the other gentlemen in the village green, where said tournament was to take place. He had been under the impression that only the gentleman of the inn would be participating, so he was surprised to find that many of the villagers had arrived to not only watch but also to take part.

As Elias Tavners stepped up to begin the day, August's ears perked at the sound of Iris' lilting voice nearby.

"Not now," she was saying in somewhat hushed tones, and when he glanced over, the man from the dance — Abernathy, he recalled — was at her side. August had seen him around the inn a time or two, but never with Iris, and he had come to believe her words that there was nothing between the two of them. Now, he questioned whether or not that thinking was correct, for the man was leaning over Iris' shoulder, a hand lightly resting on her waist as he looked over her head at what was happening in front of them.

August couldn't seem to tear his eyes away from that hand, and he was shocked when he felt his stomach tighten and a ball of jealousy begin to rise up through his throat.

The envy was similar to that which he had felt when he had seen Amelia in the arms of his best friend, which was ridiculous. He barely knew Iris Tavners whereas he and Amelia had been betrothed. It must be that he was simply jealous of the relationship the two of them shared — one which he had actually once been a part of himself.

"... lawn bowls, shuttlecock, and archery!" Elias Tavners finished exclaiming, and August realized he had not been paying the least bit of attention to anything the man had said. It seemed, however, their tournament games were now established, and teams were beginning to form.

"Overall," Tavners said, "we will hold a competition between the villagers and our boarders. Ladies and gentlemen are both welcome to take part."

August was now close enough that he could hear the conversation between Iris and Abernathy.

"*Women* are participating?" the man said with disdain and Iris nodded, a smug smile on her face.

"Yes," she said. "I told my father I would only plan such an event if we had the ability to take part as well. I see no reason why not. They are all perfectly acceptable games for ladies."

"But *with* men?"

"Yes, Ernest," she said firmly. "You will play with women. But not to worry. Violet and I will be participating with the inn's guests."

August smiled at that. He also enjoyed the fact that he would be placed against this man who clearly thought quite highly of himself.

"Come, Lord Westwood," Iris said, and he jumped, not realizing that she had even known he was there. "You and I will begin at shuttlecock."

They were participating along with Violet and Thomas

*An Earl for Iris*

Cooper. The man nodded to August before they began. August had never played with four on a side before, but he quickly found the rhythm. Players from each side batted the battledore back and forth. Once it dropped, the next player rotated in.

Iris was the first player on the team, and August was so enjoying watching her play that he nearly didn't notice when it was his turn to rotate in. Iris was laughing to such an extent that when he ran in with his racquet outstretched and his eye on the battledore, she stepped backward, not seeing him, and crashed into him, sending them sprawling together on the grassy ground beneath them.

"Oof!" he exclaimed as she landed on top of him, nearly knocking all of the air out of him. After a moment in which he caught his breath and determined that they were both fine, he became aware of just how soft were her curves atop his body. They seemed to mold into him perfectly, and when he looked up, her face so close to his, her mouth but a breath away, it took nearly all of his willpower not to lean in and take her lips within his.

But that was when he became aware of more than just her. The chatter around them had nearly gone quiet as the other players of this particular game gathered around them.

"Are you all right?" Violet asked, breaking the silence as she leaned down over them.

"I say," came a much more masculine voice that was accompanied by hands reaching down in offer to Iris. "Get up, Iris, this is embarrassing."

Iris' cheeks flamed a bright red, but it took August a moment to realize that she was not embarrassed — no, she was angry at the words coming from the man who seemed to feel he was her suitor.

She ignored the hands of Ernest Abernathy and instead

pushed herself up off of August, shifting over him as she did so.

"My apologies, Lord Westwood," she said, a smile on her face now, though whether it was for him or for the benefit of the onlookers, he wasn't entirely sure. "I became so caught up in the game that I lost where I was for a moment."

"Nothing broken," he said, standing himself and stretching his hands out as though to show her. He caught her eye, saw the spark there, and it was then that he began to laugh. After a moment, she joined in as well, and soon the group of them — with a few exceptions — joined in with a chuckle.

After an uneventful remainder of the game, they moved on to lawn bowls, a game August was certainly familiar with. He caught Iris' eye more than a time or two, and when she stood next to him as they awaited their turns, he felt the brush of her fingers against his. She kept her gaze forward, as though it was an accident, but he couldn't help the jolt of heat that shot through him, even at so innocent a touch.

Just a mild flirtation, he told himself. Nothing more. Women were not to be trusted. He had learned that from Amelia, and look at Iris — beautiful, yes, but clearly there was something between her and this Ernest Abernathy, though what, he wasn't entirely sure. She didn't seem to hold any affection for him and yet...

"How are you at archery, my lord?" she asked him with a raised eyebrow as they walked over to the next event.

He shrugged. "I enjoy it."

He was actually quite proficient, but he wasn't arrogant enough to say so.

"Shall we have a wager?" she asked with a bewitching grin.

*An Earl for Iris*

"What did you have in mind?" he asked, unable to help his intrigue.

"If I win, I can ask you whatever question I'd like and you must answer."

He wasn't so sure about that. "And if I win?"

"The same reward."

He mulled it over for a moment. He would like to know more about Abernathy, though he felt as though she may answer his questions regardless.

"Very well," he finally said, figuring that he could answer her in whatever way he'd like no matter the question — not that she would ever beat him. "You have a deal."

She nodded, and he addressed the target first. He took careful aim, and his arrow notched just next to the bull's eye. He smiled in satisfaction.

And then she stepped up, confidently picked up the bow, shot him a smile, and hit the target right in the heart.

## 9

Iris smiled triumphantly. Ever since the stable master next door had taught her to shoot years ago, she had retained her uncanny eye for hitting the target. Not that she would have told Lord Westwood that before they had their little competition.

Ernest came up behind them now.

"I hardly think this a fair competition," he said in regard to their tournament game. "Why, I'm sure the *Earl* has received private lessons since he was a child."

Iris turned to Lord Westwood to determine his reaction, and an icy hardness had glazed over his eyes as he looked at Ernest.

"Perhaps I did," he said. "But still it seems that the young lady here has bested me. The question is, will she best you as well?"

Ernest picked up the bow, closed one eye, and released the arrow. It sailed toward the target, notching in the outside circle. He threw the bow to the ground and turned to look at the two of them.

"Perhaps I am no longer interested in *archery*," he said,

*An Earl for Iris*

narrowing his eyes at Iris, and she smiled, which he apparently was not entirely expecting. But it no longer mattered what he thought of her, for her plan was complete.

Just then, Millie's father came running up, slightly out of breath.

"Iris," he said, "have you seen Millie?"

"Not since yesterday," she said, biting her lip. She liked the blacksmith and had no wish to hurt him, but at the same time, he hadn't trusted Millie enough to determine her own happiness. Iris only hoped it would all be resolved in time.

"Do you know where she might be?"

Iris took a breath. Enough time had passed that she could tell him what she knew. She and Millie had discussed this. Millie didn't want to overly worry her father and had asked Iris to tell him the truth of the matter.

"She and Burt are well enough away from here," she said, steeling her resolve. "They are to be married."

"She *what*?" the blacksmith said, his words somewhat hushed yet threatening, nonetheless.

"They are going to be married tomorrow," Iris said, standing as tall as she could with her shoulders back. "She loves Burt, Mr. Smith, as you well know, and all she longed for was to be married to him."

"This is outrageous!" Ernest cut in, standing next to Mr. Smith. "She and *I* were to be married."

"Until you became interested in this one instead," Mr. Smith said bitterly, and then the two of them turned to look at her.

"You orchestrated this, didn't you?" Mr. Smith said as he eyed her with accusation. "You, Iris Tavners, always have your nose where it doesn't belong. Stay out of my family, and stay away from Millie, do you understand me? Where is she?"

"Nearby," Iris said slowly.

"Lowestoft," he determined accurately, and Iris bit her lip.

"Come, Abernathy, perhaps we are not too late."

The two of them made for the stables next to the blacksmith shop, leaving Iris standing with Lord Westwood, Violet, and Mr. Cooper. They were all staring at her.

"Did you do this?" Violet asked. "Were they correct?"

Iris kept holding her head high. She would not feel ashamed for her actions. She had done what she felt was right, and she wouldn't apologize for it.

"Millie and I made the plan," she said, looking to Violet, willing her sister to understand. "It was what she wanted. And they won't catch them now. It's too late. We made sure of it."

"It was why you were so enthusiastic about this tournament," Violet said, her eyes widening as she realized the truth of it. "Why didn't you tell me?"

"I didn't want to involve you," Iris said with a shrug. "Then there would be no blame that could be placed upon you."

She was too nervous to look at Lord Westwood, not wanting to see the judgment in his eyes.

"Iris!"

Her father's voice boomed as it came closer and Iris cringed.

"Well," she said, attempting an air of nonchalance, "perhaps I best go see what Father would like to speak to me about. I shall see you all soon."

And at that, she practically ran away, unsure of which man she would prefer to face.

*An Earl for Iris*

~

August told himself none of this mattered as he sat in the sitting room the next evening. Why should he care anything at all as to whether or not Iris Tavners was actually involved with the son of the apothecary? It was simple village dramatics, and very soon he would be gone from here once more and Southwold and all of its inhabitants would be nothing but a memory.

But then he saw Iris from his chair near the window which overlooked the lane in front of the inn, and it was as though his feet had a mind of their own as they stood, walked out the door, and approached her. She had been looking one way and then the next as though she was searching for someone, her arms wrapped tightly around herself like she was chilled despite the warm late summer air.

"Miss Iris?" he called and she jumped, turning toward him.

"Lord Westwood," she said, a hand on her breast. "You startled me."

"So it would seem."

"And please, just call me Iris. Most people around here do.'"

"Very well," he said with a nod and then placed his hands on his hips. "Listen, I know it has nothing to do with me, but I am overcome by curiosity. Why were you allowing Abernathy to think there is something between the two of you when you clearly can't stand the man?"

She looked affronted.

"I am not sure what you mean," she said, tossing her head back ever so slightly. A couple of curls had come loose from her chignon and bounced around her shoulders with the movement.

August shook his head to clear his errant thoughts. "Come now, Iris, I am no fool," he said. "You practically cringe when he approaches, and yet he acts as though the two of you are betrothed. Why?"

"It's as you said," she said, narrowing her eyes at him ever so slightly. "It has nothing to do with you. If you really wanted to know..." her lips began to turn up in a smile, "you should have bested me at archery and you would have your question."

He had thought with all that had happened she would forget their wager, but apparently, she was much swifter than he had given her credit for.

"Consider me curious," he said with a shrug. "Has it anything to do with your friend Millie and her runaway marriage?"

She sighed and looked at him with some chagrin.

"So you have it all figured out, do you?"

"It seems that I am near the truth."

"Very well," she said, kicking the cobblestone path below her foot. "Come walk with me if you'd like and I will tell you what you are apparently so interested in knowing."

Her story was fairly succinct and August assumed she had left out a few details, but it was also understandable. Her friend Millie, the blacksmith's daughter, was to marry Abernathy but much preferred the fisherman. So Iris had captured Abernathy's attention instead.

"But the loss of Abernathy's affections did nothing to dissuade her father. And so with the tournament, all were distracted enough to allow Millie to run off with her fisherman."

"Precisely," Iris said with a smile.

*An Earl for Iris*

"Interesting," he mused and then didn't miss the look she sent his way.

"What does that mean?" she asked, and he smiled at her defensive tone.

"I simply mean that what you did for your friend is actually rather admirable — especially considering that you can hardly tolerate the man."

She paused for a moment, looking down at her feet. The afternoon was growing late and their shadows stretched out long in front of them.

"I haven't always been the best of friends to those closest to me — most especially to my sisters," she said, keeping her gaze forward and not meeting his eye. "It took Daisy and Marigold marrying and leaving the inn to make me realize how much I missed them, how much they did for me and how I, in turn... well, I have always looked after myself first, I suppose you could say. It is time I did something for someone else."

"Which is why we are here now," he murmured as he looked at the blacksmith's shop that now loomed in front of them.

"Yes," she nodded. "I have been waiting for Millie to arrive home. I know this will no longer be her home, but she loves her father so much she'll return here — if he didn't catch up with her already."

"To explain her actions."

"Yes."

"Actions you encouraged."

She rounded, finally looking him in the eye, her own gaze challenging him.

"You don't approve."

"I never said that."

"You didn't have to," she said, her hands in fists by her

side. "It doesn't matter what you think. Millie wanted to follow her heart, and she needed help to do so. It was what she wanted and I simply supported her."

"Life will be difficult, married to a fisherman, will it not?"

"Of course it will!" she said, raising her hands as though to exaggerate her point. "I told her that time and again over the last year, but still, her love for him never wavered and she will accept whatever he can and will offer her. But..." she trailed off, her expression growing wistful, "when she explained it to me, I understood. She would rather spend her life with little food on the table, but the man she loves, over plentiful cupboards with a man who would drive her mad. And trust me, that would be the least that Ernest Abernathy would do. "

"And what happens to Abernathy now?"

"Now," she said, taking a deep breath, "I will tell him how I really feel — not in so many words, but in as nice a way as I can."

They stopped in front of the blacksmith's shop, and Iris peered in the windows of the living quarters but must have found it empty for she stepped back.

"Not home yet," she murmured. "I'll keep watch."

August contemplated her, wondering how to say what he needed to without insulting her.

"Do you think that it is... proper to interfere in others' lives?"

"Lord Westwood," she said, whipping her head around to look at him. "I did what I thought was right, and I will not apologize."

August raised his hands in front of him in defense. He wanted to laugh at how passionate she had become over her

*An Earl for Iris*

own actions, but somehow he knew that would be a poor decision in the moment.

"I actually think much of what you did is admirable," he said, "as long as no one is hurt by it all."

"No one will be," she confirmed. "Millie and Burt will have their happily ever after, her father will come to realize that she will be much happier than if she had married Ernest, and Ernest, well, Ernest will be happy as long as he has himself, for that is the only person he truly cares for."

"Very well, then," he said. "You know all of these people far better than I."

"I do," she said, and then as they began to turn to back to the inn, she gasped as she looked into the distance. "They've returned!" she exclaimed, and then picked up her skirts and began to run down the cobblestones toward an approaching horse.

"Millie!" she called, and August followed along slowly, not wanting to interrupt the moment between two friends yet unable to tear himself away from this whole situation. He truly had become far too bored upon his stay here.

Millie and her Burt dismounted, and Millie wrapped her arms around Iris in an embrace.

"Thank you," he heard her exclaim as he neared them. "I could never have done this without you."

"Did your father find you?"

"He did," Millie said, "but in the end... he understood. He was there for the wedding, and I am grateful. So grateful to now have such love in my life."

He kept his distance as they spoke, and soon enough the newlyweds were continuing past him, with Iris looking on after them. It was only as he neared that he noticed the tears in her eyes.

"I was wrong," she said, and he looked at her, confused.

"About helping them?"

"No, in the past. I was wrong to put myself first so often. It feels much better to have done something for someone else, that much is for certain."

"I suppose you are right," he said with a slow nod. "I likely have much to learn from you."

"You risked yourself for your country," she said pointedly, her cheeks highlighted by the setting sun as it glowed down upon her. "One could hardly suggest that you have not put yourself first."

"It may appear that way," he said, realizing as he did so that he had not even admitted so much to himself. "But I really took my position for my own purposes — to give myself a sense of importance that I hadn't previously felt, to have the opportunity to live a life of high stakes. I love the rush, the risk. And I've only realized that now that it is gone."

"Yet you are here."

"I am here," he said.

"Very well," she said, crossing her arms over her chest and turning to look at him. "I won our wager. And now I have my question for you."

## 10

Iris didn't want to admit how handsome August looked standing in the dim remaining light of the day. She was somewhat confused as to whether or not he disapproved of her. She didn't want his opinion to matter, and yet somehow it did — far more than even her father's, who had been irate, of course. But it all paled in comparison to the glow on Millie's face when she returned to Southwold, newly married.

Iris had been contemplating which question she would put to Lord Westwood. She knew he expected her to ask why he was back at the inn, and while of course she was curious, there was another question she now felt the need to ask, despite the fact she knew he would far prefer she didn't.

"Very well," he said, his expression turning wary, and he leaned back against the brick wall of the general store, where they now stood beside. It was the last building before the village ended and the marshes and fields beyond began. "I am assuming you'd like to know why I am here?"

"I would be pleased for you to tell me that, but that is not my question."

He stayed silent, waiting for her to speak.

"What happened," she asked softly, "between you and the woman you said you were returning to? The one with whom you had thought to spend the rest of your life?"

He narrowed his eyes as his typically jovial mouth turned downward in a scowl.

"I have no wish to speak of it," he said, turning from her to begin back down the path, but she caught his arm with one hand.

"We made a wager," she said, her eyes holding his in a challenge. "I expect you to honor it."

"And I expect you to keep your curiosity just that — curiosity," he retorted. "What does it even matter?"

"It just... does," she said gently, and it was the right tactic, for his anger lessened ever so slightly, and he gave a crisp nod.

"Fine," he said, dropping his hands and leaning in toward her as though to intimidate her, but Iris was no coward. "You would really like to know? I returned to London expecting to find her awaiting me with open arms. I hadn't even stopped at my own townhouse before I went to her father's, so eager was I to see her. I was informed she was not there — but could be found at the home of Lord Bollingbrook. Which was interesting, for Lord Bollingbrook was my closest friend. I told myself they must be commiserating, that they each surely had missed me to so great an extent that they were finding comfort with one another."

A sick feeling began to grow in Iris' stomach as she realized to where this story was leading.

"You don't have to continue," she said, her voice just over a whisper, but it was far too late now.

"Oh no, you wanted to know," he insisted, and she swallowed hard. "They found comfort all right. When I knocked

*An Earl for Iris*

on the door and asked for her, the butler frowned at me and asked if I was referring to *Lady* Bollingbrook."

He chuckled sardonically now, and Iris bit her lip. She never should have asked this. She had allowed her curiosity to overcome all else, as she always did. So much for putting others' best interests first.

"I was shown into the drawing room. There, I had to witness the two of them fawning over one another and telling me how they had spent so much time together and eventually 'just couldn't help themselves.' It was sickening."

"I'm so sorry," she whispered, and he shrugged.

"It's over now. Done. I now know how fickle the affections of a woman can be, and I will not make such a mistake again."

"Not all women are the same," she insisted, it suddenly becoming imperative that he understand and not believe such a thing.

"How do you think your Ernest will feel once you tell him the truth?"

"I do not think he will overly mind," she said honestly, "for he cares for no one but himself."

"Isn't that what you said about yourself? And yet you would feel betrayed, would you not?"

His words sunk in and a sense of shame swept over Iris. He was right. She hadn't overly considered Ernest's feelings because he was... well, Ernest.

"You are right," she said. "I will tell him how I feel as soon as possible... and as gently as I possibly can, I promise."

She paused for a moment.

"Do you still love her? Your Amelia?"

"Does it matter?"

Yes, suddenly it mattered very much.

"No. I was just wondering."

"No, I no longer love her," he said bitterly. "The worst of it is that I don't think I ever really did. It was the betrayal that hurt the most. Both hers and the man who had been my friend for twenty years. I'm angry, Iris. Just angry."

"Anger doesn't suit you," she said, "perhaps forgiveness would be best."

"Perhaps in time," he said, turning to look at her once more. "I should go. Good luck with Abernathy."

She nodded and watched him stride away with a knot of worry in the pit of her stomach. He was a proud man, one who would never want to admit any failings.

But her worry would have to wait until later. For at the moment, there was a conversation that needed to be finished as soon as possible. With a man she had no desire to have it with.

Fortunately, the apothecary was empty save for Ernest himself when she arrived.

"Iris!" he said with his sickly smooth smile. "What a surprise. You have managed to leave your duties at the inn?"

"Yes," she said. "With the tournament today, everything had been prepared ahead of time for the evening meal. I must return soon to serve, but otherwise, most of the men are still drinking in the dining area."

"How nice for them," he said, "to not have to return to work like the rest of us."

"I suppose they spent enough time risking their lives that they deserve a bit of a break," she said with a shrug, and he snorted, reminding her of why she could never be with a man like him.

"We are alone here, you do realize that," he said now, leaning over the counter with a smile on his face. "Is that why you came here to seek me out — so that perhaps we might come to know one another better... in another sense?"

"No," she said immediately, shivering as she did. She couldn't imagine such a thing with a man like Ernest. "I am, however, glad that we have a moment to ourselves. I must talk to you about something of some importance."

"Good," he said, moving the bottles to one side of the counter in front of him and rounding it to the same side she was on. "I also think it is time we discuss how we might further our relationship."

"That's just it," Iris said, wringing her hands together. "I actually... I have no wish to do so."

"Pardon me?"

"I am sorry, Ernest," she said, her words coming out quickly now. "I do hope you will understand, but after spending some time together, I believe that we actually do not suit one another very well. Perhaps we should move on, find others we would be better with."

His forehead creased, his eyes narrowed, his mouth forming a thin line as he stepped closer to her.

"Tell me, Iris," he said, his voice low and gruff, "Does this have anything to do with the Earl who recently came to town? Because, let me tell you, the man will never have time or interest in you for anything more than a brief dalliance. He would ruin you and then leave. Or... does this have anything to do with your friend Millie?"

Iris bit her lip.

"It has nothing to do with any of that, Ernest," she lied. "It is just that you and I... well, you would become tired of me after a time, I'm sure of it, and I feel that perhaps we just would be happier were we not together, that is all."

"Oh you think that, do you?" he said, and every time he

took a step toward her, she took one backward. "Perhaps I can convince you otherwise."

"I really don't think—"

But then her back came up against the counter behind her and she had nowhere to move. He took the opportunity to practically pounce upon her, his mouth coming down hard on hers as she fought to escape. She tried to duck, but one of his hands held her in place. She reared her head back long enough to emit a scream for help, but he quickly silenced her with the other hand over her mouth. Iris fought like a wildcat, but he was much stronger than she was, and soon he was fumbling with her skirts. She took all of the strength within her and jerked her knee up as hard as she could between his legs. He emitted a howl but didn't let go, and she nearly lost all hope — until the door of the apothecary banged open and August stormed in, anger filling his face as he took in the scene in front of him.

"Get off her," he snarled, and Ernest chuckled.

"Oh, but she wants it," he said, and with his attention otherwise occupied, Iris lifted her hand back and connected her fist solidly with his nose.

He cried out and released her as his hands came to his face, catching the blood, and Iris stepped back in shock over all that just happened — and the pain that was radiating from her fist up through her arm.

August took a step toward the man as though he was going to further hurt him, but Iris held up a hand, shaking her head.

"Let's just go," she said, and despite his hesitation, August nodded and placed an arm around her waist to help her to the door. They were about to leave when he turned back for one final word.

"If you ever try anything like this again," he threatened

*An Earl for Iris*

Ernest, "I do not care where I am or what else may be occurring in my life, but I will come back and end yours. Do you hear me?"

Ernest was now holding the bottom of his shirt to his nose, but he managed a quick nod, though his eyes remained hard and focused on the two of them.

"Good," August said, and then before Iris knew what was happening, he had her out the door and away from the apothecary, a place she knew she would never again enter.

## 11

August kept a firm grip around Iris as he walked her away from the apothecary and down the street back toward the inn. She was shaking something fierce, but as he pulled her tightly toward him, he realized that he was trembling nearly as violently.

He couldn't explain what had drawn him toward Iris and the apothecary. After they had parted, he had intended to return to the inn, to forget Iris and the drama that seemed to surround her. But then an itch had bothered him, one that told him that he wasn't done with her, that he still had a role to play and that she might need him.

When he had opened the door to the apothecary and taken in the sight before him, he had nearly gone blind with a rage unlike any he had known before.

It was clear that the embrace was not one welcomed by both sides. He only wished that he could have planted his fist in the man's face before Iris beat him to it, although if anyone had the right to do so, it was she.

She stopped suddenly now, placing her hands on his arms.

"I don't want to go back to the inn," she said, and he read the desperation in her eyes. "Not yet, not right now. Please?"

"Where would you like to go?"

"Anywhere without people," she said. "The beach, perhaps?"

"Which way?" he asked simply, willing to do whatever she wished at the moment as long as it would help her to feel better.

She pointed, and he took her arm once more, leading her down the path toward the sandy shore.

"Does your hand hurt?" he asked, looking down at it, and she nodded tersely.

"Come," he said, and led her to the edge of the sand, placing her hand in the cool sea water. "Does that feel better?" he asked, and she nodded once more.

August yearned to do nothing more than to take her in his arms and tell her everything would be fine, but he wasn't entirely sure how she would feel if he did such a thing, and he also didn't know that it would be the truth to say so. For he could be gone on the morrow, and she would be left here, living just down the road from Ernest Abernathy. Iris had proven she could protect herself to an extent, but if he hadn't arrived when he did... he didn't want to think of what could have happened.

"Are you all right?" he asked her, and she just stared at him for a moment, facing him now, her uninjured hand coming to grip his upper arm as she held on tightly as though he were her anchor to maintaining control.

"Yes. No. I... I'm not entirely sure."

She paused for a moment, her gaze on the sea before it returned to him.

"Lord Westwood..."

"August."

"August, then. Thank you... for coming when you did. Ernest has always been a rather arrogant sort, but I never thought he would do... would try... what he did."

"Sometimes one never knows the true nature of a man until it is too late."

She wiped a hand over her face, though he hadn't seen any tears trickle down.

"It was my fault."

"Your fault?"

"I flirted with him, made him think I was interested."

"But you told him no, did you not, when it came to...?"

"Of course!" she exclaimed with wide eyes, and he looked intently at her.

"Then Iris, it was not your fault," he said. "A man should never take a woman unwillingly."

She nodded, but he wasn't entirely sure that she believed him.

"August..." she said, her voice just above a whisper now. "Will you... will you hold me?"

"Gladly," he said, and then without pausing to think he wrapped his arms around her and held her close.

She fit perfectly in his arms and when he leaned in, he could smell the lavender in her hair, the lemon soap she must use radiating up from her body. He was glad, at that moment, that it was him offering her comfort and no one else.

And then he realized the truth. He wanted her to be his. Possessiveness filled him as he held her in his arms, and he longed to tilt her head up and take her lips, but after what she had just been through, now certainly wasn't the time.

She seemed so delicate wrapped in his arms, and despite how perfect she felt within them, after a minute or so had

*An Earl for Iris*

passed, he knew he should let her go. And yet still she clung to him in equal measure.

"Iris?" he finally said, hearing the huskiness of his own voice, and he cleared his throat. "Are you all right?"

"I am," she said, leaning back away from him but not quite letting go. "I'm sorry," she said. "I shouldn't have asked this of you."

"I am happy you did."

They stood there, looking at one another, her crystal-blue eyes piercing into his. What was he doing? He had told himself that he would never trust another woman, that it would be wrong to allow anyone else into his heart. So why did this feel so right?

She tentatively reached an arm up, her fingers coming to his cheek, ever so lightly brushing against it before she reached her other hand up to cup his face.

"Iris," he said again, though this time more in question than anything else. He wanted nothing more than to kiss her, but he couldn't be the one to initiate it, he wouldn't. He would wait, as long as she wanted him to, so that she would know this time, he wouldn't turn her away.

She stood on the tips of her toes, her face lifting to his, and he leaned in ever so slightly. When their lips were but a breath away from one another, he paused, resting his forehead against hers.

"Are you sure?" he asked, and she nodded against his head.

"I've never been more sure," she said, and then she closed the gap between them, her soft, pillowy lips coming to his.

August nearly fell backward at the contact. It was as though a shock of lightning had streaked down from the sky, hitting him and sending a jolt of energy through his entire being. He'd thought he had loved Amelia, but never had her touch left him feeling quite like this. It was thrilling, it was shocking, it was — terrifying.

For it was opening himself up to the potential of being rejected once more. This was a woman who had more than likely broken a few hearts in her time, and he had no wish to be her latest conquest. Before Amelia he would never have doubted himself; he would have been sure that a woman could never reject a man like him — he was the one who'd had his selection of women prior to Amelia. But now everything had changed and he was filled with doubt.

But that doubt was becoming overrun with his feelings for Iris. Now that he had her, he didn't know how he could be without her.

What had begun as an innocent kiss, their lips lightly teasing one another, was now deepening, though whether he initiated it or she, he had no idea. It was as though they were of one mind, on the same level. His lips moved over hers in abandon, and then his tongue swept inside her mouth, tasting, teasing, as they came to know one another somehow more intimately than if they were actually making love.

This was madness. But madness that he never wanted to end.

Finally, however, they eased back away from one another, and it seemed as though her eyes were glistening.

"I'm sorry," he managed.

"Whatever for?" she asked, her eyes sparkling. "I believe I was the one who sought this out... sought *you* out. Perhaps I shouldn't have..."

She bit her lip, and for just a moment she displayed the slightest bit of hesitation, of the same worry, perhaps, that he was feeling, and he quickly put her concerns to rest.

*An Earl for Iris*

"You certainly should have," he said, one corner of his lips quirking into a smile as he stared at her flushed cheeks and now red lips, knowing he was the one who had caused her to look as she did. "I simply did not want to cause you any further distress."

"Far from it," she assured him, her lips now turning up in a sultry smile. "You have overcome his touch and instead left me with the memory of yours. Thank you."

He chuckled then, soft and low. "Happy to oblige, love."

The word slipped off his tongue before he even realized it, and while her eyes flew up to meet his when she heard it, she said nothing to acknowledge it, for which he was grateful.

"I best be returning now," she said softly, though August sensed that she longed to remain here as much as he did. She stepped away from him, but he didn't let go.

"Iris," he said, retaining his hold on her hand.

"Yes?"

He didn't exactly know what to say, only that he didn't want her to leave him.

"Promise me you'll be careful?" he settled for instead. "Do not allow yourself to be alone... especially when Abernathy might be about."

For some reason, she looked somewhat disappointed, but she nodded. "Of course," she said, "I can look after myself."

Which was entirely what he was afraid of — that she would be far too confident and let her guard down.

"Please?" he said, knowing he sounded somewhat desperate, but she nodded.

"Very well," she said with a slight smile, "I promise not to be alone."

He wished he could be the one who would always be

with her, who would ensure that she was always protected. But to allow her in, to open his heart to her once more... he wasn't entirely sure if he could.

～

As much as she wanted to break into a run, Iris forced herself to walk slowly back to the house, a wave of both euphoria and exhaustion overcoming her after the swing of emotions she had experienced throughout the day. She brought a hand to her lips, still feeling the pressure of August's upon hers. Oh, what had she done? She could tell herself that she had simply needed comfort, that she had to wash away Ernest's touch with another's, but she knew she was lying.

When August had entered the apothecary's shop, relief beyond anything she had ever felt had flooded through her. For it was not just the fact that he had helped rescue her; it was the knowledge that his presence brought about such comfort, such assurance that all would be fine. That as long as he was there, she didn't have to worry.

Which was ridiculous. She hardly knew the man. Yet... she loved him. How she could, she had no idea, but it was a sensation beyond just the superficial. She had been attracted to others before, of course, had loved to flirt and tease and attract men of all sorts. But with August, she knew if — when — he left, her entire world would fall apart.

Which was exactly why she should never have allowed this to be.

She sighed as she entered the inn, closing the door behind her and leaning against it, as though drawing strength from the wood of the building that was both her home and her prison. For she had longed to escape for years but now the thought was daunting. What was she to do? What was she to say to August? If she told him how she felt, it was just as likely he would reject her as he had before. She was sure he had simply felt sorry for her, that he had returned her kiss because to deny her again after her experience with Ernest would be an ultimate rejection.

Iris wiped her hand over her face and pushed away from the door, hearing a low murmur of voices. Where was it coming from? She should really forget it, should see to her duties, should concentrate on all of her own worries, including not only August but the fact that the Abernathys were prominent in town and Ernest lived just down the street.

But old habits were difficult to overcome. And so she continued down the hall on her tiptoes, ears alert. If she happened to overhear something as she walked by a door, it wasn't her fault, was it?

## 12

August slowly followed Iris back to the inn, wanting to give her time to enter before him. Goodness, he had no idea what he was supposed to do now. He had no thought as to how much longer he would remain here at the inn. And how was he supposed to treat her after all that had happened? Would she expect more from him? Would she tell her family of what had happened? He ran his hand through his hair. He would be worried that Tavners might ask him to leave, but from what he knew of the man, it was more likely he would be hoping that August would marry this daughter as well.

As for whether he ever could... if she betrayed him, as could very likely happen, then he would have to spend the rest of his life attached to her, which he didn't think he could ever manage.

The worst part about it was that this was all his own doing.

He pushed open the door of the inn, wandering down toward his sitting room until it was time for the late dinner.

*An Earl for Iris*

It had been a long day, and he could use a drink. He was just passing by a small alcove near the front entryway when he nearly ran into something — or someone.

"Ouch!" came a soft cry from his feet, and he leaned down, confused.

"Iris?"

"Shh," she hissed, before waving him down to crouch next to her.

"What *are* you doing?" he asked, but she placed a hand over his mouth. He surprised her by kissing it, and when her eyes widened he winked — he just couldn't help himself.

"I'm listening," she whispered and pressed her ear back against the keyhole.

He stared at her, shocked.

"Who are you spying on?" he asked, not wanting to let her see how intrigued he was. He didn't want to admit it, but he rather liked learning what happened behind closed doors. It was part of why he had enjoyed his role.

"Violet," she whispered. "And Thomas Cooper."

Well, that was interesting. Violet had struck him as a bit of a wallflower, and he wondered at Cooper's interest in her. But everyone had a preference, and he was glad the man hadn't set his sights on Iris.

"What are they doing?" he asked, and she put a finger to her lips once more. Suddenly her eyes grew large and she stood abruptly, grabbing his hand and pulling her with him as she tugged him down the hallway and into the sitting room.

She shut the door and turned to August, giggling.

"That was close!" she exclaimed, and he raised an eyebrow.

"Do you make it a habit of listening at keyholes?"

Her cheeks reddened.

"I, ah, have tried to lessen the practice as of late," she said, biting her lip, and he longed to lean in and kiss it. "My father says I have always been far too curious."

"Curiosity can be both an admirable trait as well as one to watch out for."

"Yes, well..." She shrugged. "My father has never been one to share much with us, so I began to discover things on my own."

"But it was not your father you were spying on this evening."

"No," she said, shaking her head. "In fact—"

But her words were cut short when the door opened behind her, nearly knocking into her, and Thomas Cooper walked in.

Damn. August had actually been somewhat interested in what she would have to say about the man, but he supposed he would have to wait until another time to learn more.

"Lord Westwood, Miss Iris," the blond man greeted them, looking from one of them to the other, as though questioning what they might be doing here together — which was rather ironic considering he had previously been ensconced with another Tavners daughter. "Quite an interesting day today, was it not?"

"It was," Iris nodded. Then, in a manner that was not at all usual for her, she said, "Please excuse me," and was out the door without a backward glance.

Cooper leaned back against the wall, folding his arms across his chest with a knowing smile on his face as he looked at August.

"Do you have an interest in this particular Tavners

*An Earl for Iris*

woman, then? I can see why. She's a beauty. But a might too... *brash* for my liking."

August stiffened at the insult.

"She is friendly, is all. If you find her brash it is simply because she is attempting to make you feel welcome here."

Cooper chuckled.

"Does she do that with all of the gentlemen guests?"

"Now, listen here—"

"Not to worry, Westwood, I have no interest in stealing your woman. In fact, I find the other Tavners girl much more to my liking. Now, tell me, you've been here a time or two before. What is one to do for amusement around here?"

August shrugged. "Walking, card games, reading. It's a quiet village, that is for certain."

"Perhaps one day you can show me some of the sights."

"Very well," August said, though he found it somewhat of an odd request, "though I'm sure Miss Violet may be interested in accompanying you."

"I thought you and I could get to know one another better seeing as how we could be here for some time," Cooper responded. "Tell me of your effort in the war. What brings you here?"

August walked to the sideboard and poured himself a drink to give himself a moment to determine just what he should tell Cooper. The man had obviously been a soldier of some type himself, but August had no idea what his role had been.

"I was intelligence," he finally said, pouring a drink for Cooper now and handing it to him, "and yourself?"

"The same," Cooper said, which August found surprising. "Where did you find yourself?"

"In France," August said, not interested in sharing

anything further until he knew more about Cooper, "and you?"

"I was in the enemy camp in Portugal," Cooper said, clearly not having such inhibitions himself. "I came across a piece of vital information that I must guard with my life."

"I see," August said. "That is why you are in hiding?"

"In hiding?"

"Yes," August said slowly, wondering at why the man would sound somewhat surprised. "That is why we are all at The Wild Rose Inn, is it not?"

"Of course," Cooper responded smoothly, taking a sip of his drink, "what has caused you to hide?"

"It seems that I may know something I am not supposed to," August said pointedly. "Which, I do not. All I managed to do was have myself some fun."

"Were you at court then? How intriguing. You must have a good story or two."

"I'm sorry to disappoint, but there is not much to tell."

Cooper eyed him shrewdly but said nothing else, and a sense of unease began to crawl up August's spine.

"I think I am going in for that cold dinner we were promised," August said. "I find myself rather hungry."

Cooper nodded and tipped his drink to August, who responded in kind and continued on his way.

∼

"Violet?" Iris stepped into the kitchen, where Violet was laying out the previously prepared food for that night's late dinner.

"There you are," Violet said, turning her head to Iris. "I was wondering if you had decided to leave everything to me while you were off with your lord."

*An Earl for Iris*

Iris raised her eyebrows at the slight abrasiveness to her sister's tone.

"I hardly think that is fair," she said, and Violet shrugged.

"You have been spending a fair bit of time with him as of late."

"I still see to all of my duties," Iris defended herself. "Besides that, you and Mr. Cooper seem to be awfully friendly as well."

"I'm not sure what you mean."

"No?" Iris asked with a raised eyebrow. "Has he not found stolen moments alone with you? Asked you all sorts of things about the inn, the family, or guests?"

Violet whirled around, narrowing her eyes at Iris.

"You've been spying on me."

"I wouldn't call it spying," Iris said carefully. "I am simply looking out for you."

"Listening in at keyholes is not looking out for someone," Violet responded, and Iris was shocked at her usually mild-mannered sister. "Really, Iris, it is time you grew up."

"Excuse me?"

"I do not follow you and Lord Westwood around. Why can you not allow me the same privilege of privacy?"

"I do not mean to fight with you, Violet, nor to spy on you," Iris said with a sigh as she wrapped a cool wet cloth around her hand. "It is just that... there is something about Mr. Cooper. Something that I do not trust. I only want to make sure he doesn't take advantage of you."

"What do you mean, you do not trust him?"

"He became interested in you from the moment he walked through the door of the inn, and I can't explain it, but I just get this feeling when I am around him that something is... not right."

Violet placed her hands on her hips and leaned back against the table behind her.

"I cannot believe you, Iris."

"Whatever do you mean?"

"You are jealous."

"Of Mr. Cooper? Not at all!" Iris exclaimed. While the man may be handsome, she was not attracted to him in the least.

"You may not want him for yourself, but you are jealous that he has taken an interest in me instead of you," Violet said, her purple-blue eyes now slightly tearing up and Iris' heart broke a little that her sister would think such a thing of her. "You cannot imagine that a man might actually want me and not you."

"Oh, Violet, that is not it at all!" Iris exclaimed. "Do you not wonder at why he was asking you so many questions? Why does he want to know the comings and goings of guests, of who has previously stayed and who we anticipate may be coming in the future? Why does it matter?"

"Perhaps it is simply that he is interested in my life!" Violet said, a tear escaping now and she brushed it aside. "Why is that so hard to believe?"

"It isn't, Violet, not at all," Iris said. "In fact, I can think of no other woman who is as loving and as wonderful as you, truly I do not. You know I am a good judge of character, that you cannot deny. Please, think whatever you want of me, but be careful, will you not?"

"As you always are?" Violet said now, turning back to her task as though she could no longer stand speaking to Iris. "I will be fine, Iris, do not worry about me. You can keep your attention on Lord Westwood."

"I'm sorry, Violet," Iris said softly. "I didn't mean to offend you. I was concerned, that was all."

"Please stop your listening at keyholes as well," Violet said. "It is hardly becoming for a woman of your age."

Iris nodded despite the fact that Violet couldn't see her, and dashed a tear from her own eye before moving forward to help Violet, in silence.

## 13

"Iris!" August called, pleased to find her sitting out on the sandy shore when he began his walk the next morning. "How are you today?"

She turned to look at him and sighed dramatically when he sat down next to her. "Not overly well, I'm afraid."

"No?" he asked, concerned about her after yesterday. "'Tis understandable after what happened."

"It isn't that — thanks to you. It's actually my sister, Violet," she said. "Of all of us, she is usually the peaceful sort, not one to ever hold a grudge or suspect anything suspicious of anyone. However, I am only trying to look out for her, and she believes I have other motives."

"What do you mean?"

"It's about Mr. Cooper," Iris said, turning to him at last, her hands upon her knees. "He took an interest in Violet the moment he arrived here. It's not that I don't understand why. There is just something about him that seems rather suspicious, and then when I was listening yesterday, he was asking a great deal about her usual movements in a day as well as those of our guests. Violet says he is simply interested in her, but I am not sure I believe it."

"He does ask a lot of questions," August said, treading carefully, for he had no desire to enter into an argument between two sisters.

"Doesn't he, though?" Iris said. "The moment I met him, something seemed off. The look he gave me, well, it was not what I am used to."

"No?" August asked, a twinge of jealousy beginning to stir in his stomach. "And just what are you used to?"

Iris' cheeks turned pink. "I do find that men are typically... interested in me," she said, looking out at the sea for a moment. "Not that I need them to be, nor do I expect it. He, however, hardly looked my way. When he did, it was as though he was... mocking me."

"Perhaps he simply has a different preference."

"Of course he could," Iris said, her eyes sparking. "It is just not the feeling I have. Violet thinks I am jealous that he would be interested in her instead of me, but of course, that is not the case."

"He is a good-looking man," August said, wondering if, perhaps, her sister had touched on the truth.

"That matters nothing!" Iris said vehemently. "Besides that... you know that it is you I far prefer."

August regarded her for a moment. He wanted to believe her words, truly he did. But all she had just told him led him, for a moment, to question whether there was more to it. He couldn't deny that Cooper also caused him to feel a slight bit of unease after his inquiries into August's actions. Iris would know nothing about the war effort or what could be at play, however, so she could hardly have the same explanation. She was also a woman who enjoyed the attention of gentlemen. Perhaps she was becoming bored with him already.

"I'd like to think so," he finally responded to her words, and she looked up at him, her eyes narrowing a touch.

"You sound as though you do not believe me," she said, raising her voice ever so slightly above the wind and the sound of the waves beyond her.

He sighed, looking over her shoulder at the peaceful scenery beyond, his swirling emotions at war.

"I would like to believe you."

"You do not?" she asked incredulously.

"Experience has told me that I should be careful," he said slowly. "I am not saying that I do not trust you. You must understand, however, after the past, that I might be wary."

Iris quickly came to her feet, her eyes stormy as she glared at him. "Why does no one believe anything I have to say?"

"I just explained—"

"It's fine, I understand," she said abruptly. "Apparently my own past speaks for me. I must go."

"Iris—"

But it was too late. She was gone.

~

IRIS IGNORED everyone she encountered as she ran into the inn and straight up to her bedchamber. She pulled out a piece of vellum and her pen and ink and began to scribble away. Daisy was too far away to help, but there was someone else to whom she could turn. And while her sister Daisy was practical, when it came to matters of the heart, she knew Marigold would know what to do. She had to — for Iris had no idea what her next action would be.

~

It was but a week later when Iris' plea was answered.

She was sitting — alone — in the family quarters darning socks and had just pricked herself with the needle.

"Ouch!" she said as a bit of blood welled up, and she had brought her finger to her mouth when a knock on the door caused her to jump. "Who is it?" she called, her voice muffled.

The door opened to reveal Marigold standing there smiling at her, and Iris jumped up and raced toward her sister, enveloping her in a hug.

"Oh, Marigold, I am so glad to see you!"

Marigold laughed. "I do not think I ever would have anticipated such exuberance from you over seeing me at the inn," she said. "But I'll take it."

Iris looked over her shoulder to see that the Marquess of Dorchester, Marigold's husband, stood in the hallway looking as uncomfortable as he ever did. He was a rather gloomy sort, but Marigold loved him as much as he loved her in turn. While Iris didn't understand the attraction and had taken some time to come to know Lord Dorchester, she was pleased about her sister's marriage regardless.

Even if it meant that her sister now resided elsewhere.

"Hello, my lord," she called with a smile, and Lord Dorchester nodded at her.

"I hope you are well, Iris," he said, then looked between the sisters. "I shall go see that our things are unpacked."

"Thank you, Jacob," Marigold said, turning to him with a warm smile that Iris had also seen upon the face of her sister Daisy. It was a smile of love. A pang of pain suddenly cut through her chest. Would she ever know the same with a man? One man in particular? She blinked back the tears that threatened at the thought of being denied it, but when she turned to Marigold, she saw that her perceptive sister was aware that something was amiss.

And, well, there had been that letter.

"Come," Marigold said, closing the door and then taking Iris' hand to lead her back to the sofa. "Tell me what the trouble is."

So Iris did. She told Marigold of Lord Westwood's return, of the fact that she had feelings for him that she couldn't shake, that Lord Westwood had been cuckolded by his fiancée and now, between his own experience and his knowledge of Iris' past, wouldn't trust her. She told Marigold of Thomas Cooper and his apparent connection with Violet, of her own suspicions, and how both Violet and Lord Westwood had reacted to them.

Marigold listened to it all with her usual reserved patience, simply nodding and allowing Iris to tell the tale.

"And now?" she asked, and Iris looked up at her with question.

"What do you mean?"

"Since this all happened," Marigold said. "What has occurred since then?"

Iris shrugged and looked down at her finger. The tiny prick was unnoticeable, though she still had a crack in her knuckle from where it had connected with Ernest's nose.

"Violet only speaks to me when necessary, and when she does, it is with extreme politeness. More than anything, I feel badly that I have hurt her, though in truth, Marigold, I was only looking out for her best interests — you must believe me."

*An Earl for Iris*

Marigold nodded. "I do."

"And as for Lord Westwood... I apologized for reacting so dramatically, and we do converse but nothing is at all the same between us. It is nearly the same politeness that exists between me and Violet, and Marigold, you know that I am not one who responds well to such coldness."

"No, you do not," Marigold said, and Iris could tell she was doing all she could to keep from laughing at her but she let it go.

"So what do I do?" Iris asked helplessly. "How do I make everything right with Violet, how do I look out for her if she doesn't want me to, and what do I do about all that I feel for Lord Westwood?"

Marigold took Iris' hands in hers, and Iris felt comforted by the ocean of Marigold's deep blue eyes that stared deeply into her own.

"Those are deep questions," she said with a slight chuckle, and then she sighed. "I do wish Daisy were here to help us answer them."

"She lives much farther away. Besides, I thought you might be more valuable, for this is a matter of the heart," Iris said, and Marigold raised her eyebrows as she smiled at her sister.

"Oh, so I wasn't your only option!" she teased.

"Well, I still chose you," Iris said practically and Marigold waved a hand in the air.

"I am only jesting," she said. "Now, as for your dilemma..." She paused for a moment in thought. "Violet will come around, you know that. None of us have remained angry at one another for long spans of time. I know you want to look out for her, Iris. That is quite lovely of you, but there is little you can do, as she is a grown woman now and a smart one at that."

"But she is so innocent," Iris protested. "And she is a romantic, always believing the best of people and sure that love will always win out, when in fact that is not always the case."

She eyed her sister. "Which is not helped by the love that you and Daisy have found with your noble husbands."

"For that, I will not apologize," Marigold said. She sat back, contemplating Iris.

"What is it?" Iris asked.

"Do you truly think this Thomas Cooper is not to be trusted?"

"I'm sure of it," Iris said. "I have no idea why, but I just feel it."

"Well, you are usually right about these things," Marigold said, tilting her head in contemplation. "I will ask Jacob his thoughts on the man as well. In the meantime, I see no problem in watching the two of them, but say no more to Violet as it will only further upset her."

"That's a good point," Iris said. "As for Lord Westwood… what do I do?"

Marigold smiled. "That's an easy one," she said. "Just follow your heart."

## 14

Follow your heart. They were the same words Iris had given Millie, but the advice somehow seemed more difficult when applied to herself. All Marigold had added was that Iris would understand when the time was right. Her words were far too cryptic for Iris' liking. She would prefer someone to tell her something straight out, as she herself liked to receive information. But Marigold had been resolute.

At least her appearance had somewhat helped Violet warm up to her once more, as Marigold eased the strain between them. Iris was still careful to say nothing about Thomas Cooper, though she watched him carefully. There was, however, nothing untoward about his actions over the next couple of days.

Iris was dressing one morning when through her bedroom window she saw August walking down to the beach. She remembered when he first arrived he had told her how he was going to make such strolls into a daily habit. She hadn't believed him at first, but here he was, weeks later, following through. He was a man of his word, something she appreciated.

Should she follow him this morning? No. She shouldn't. She really shouldn't. But Iris hated leaving anything unresolved, and perhaps it was best to simply have a discussion.

Dressed in one of her favorite morning dresses, a lavender creation — one she wouldn't typically work in and therefore one of her betters — she stepped out the door of the inn. She saw that wasn't the only one who'd had the idea to follow August. Thomas Cooper was walking ahead of her. What could he be up to?

She followed them along the beach, slowing when she neared them. The men had their backs to her now as they looked out at the ocean beyond.

"...afternoon, then?"

"That will be fine."

"Excellent. I shall see you then."

Iris took a step backward as Mr. Cooper then turned, coming to a sudden halt when he saw her standing there.

"Miss Iris," he greeted her, causing August to turn around, his face remaining stoic when he saw her.

"Mr. Cooper," she said, nodding when he continued on by her before she greeted August.

"August," she said, her voice just above a whisper. She wished she knew what he was thinking. She wanted to ask him what he and Mr. Cooper had been speaking about, but she was aware that she had already caused enough havoc when it came to the man.

"Iris," he responded, his hands clasped behind his back. "How are you?"

"Just fine," she said, hating this stilted politeness between them. "And you?"

*An Earl for Iris*

"Fine," he said. "You must be pleased your sister is home."

"Very much so," she said, smiling before becoming wistful. "It's funny. I encouraged her to look for love, to find a man to marry. I just never realized how much I would miss her until she left."

"That is often the case," he acknowledged. "We can be quite surprised."

"I'm sorry," she said suddenly. "I shouldn't have said such a thing after what you went through."

"Actually," he said. "That wasn't to what I was referring."

"Oh," Iris said, feeling her cheeks warm. "You... you do not say."

"I do not," he said, his expression much more serious than usual. "Iris, I'm not sure how much longer I will remain here, but at some point in time I will be returning to my life."

"I know," she said, a heavy weight in her chest at the thought.

"I do not like the way things have been between us over the past week or so," he said, releasing his arms in front of him now. "I know you believe that I do not trust you. You must understand that it is more that I do not know *how* to trust again. But maybe... we need to try again. What do you think?"

"I... am not entirely sure. I do wish for us to be friendly once more, but August, there is also the fact that I have never wanted to be a man's second choice. When you were last here, you hardly even looked at me."

He took her hands in his.

"I know that it might appear that way, and I understand, truly I do," he said, looking down at where their hands were joined before returning to her face. "But Iris, to me, loyalty is paramount. In addition, what I have come to realize is that I was so fixated on what I thought was the path of my life, the woman I was to be with, that I lost sight of who she was and more fell in love with the idea of being married to her than the woman herself. With you... it is only you that I see. So what do you say? May we start over?"

Iris felt her heart melting at his words.

"I think we could try that," she said, a slow smile breaking out on her face. "Truly I do. And as for Thomas Cooper..."

"He seems fairly harmless to me, though I must agree that there is something rather off about him," August said. "Let me determine what that might be, all right?"

"How do you propose to do that?" she asked, raising an eyebrow.

"I have greater means to do so than you," he said, releasing her hands and tapping her on the nose with an index finger. "I was a spy, remember?"

She did, though that didn't make her any happier to leave the task to him when she knew she would likely have made as great a spy as had ever lived. She sensed, however, that now wasn't the time to tell him of such a thought.

"Very well," she said, "but do you promise to tell me of whatever you learn?"

"You know there is no reason I should have to do so, do you not?"

"Of course," she said, "I am simply asking."

"You are a difficult woman to deny," he said with a sigh, then hesitantly reached a hand out in front of him. "Would you join me for my walk?"

"I would," she said, smiling up at him as she twined her fingers with his, her heart practically glowing within her chest.

*An Earl for Iris*

∼

August could feel the imprint of every one of her fingers against his hand. He had missed Iris over the past week, but he had questioned whether or not he had any right to approach her after he had practically accused her of being the same type of woman as Amelia. But it seemed she was, thank goodness, the forgiving sort.

"Come," she said, tugging at his hand. "You have walked this beach one time too many. I'll take you somewhere else."

"Intriguing," he said, winking at her. "Though I have come to rather enjoy this beach."

"Are you not a man who appreciates something new now and again?"

"You have come to know me too well, Iris," he said with a grin. "What would make you surmise such?"

"You are an Earl who went to work for the Crown as a spy," she said, throwing a shrewd glance his way. "What reason would you have to do such a thing?"

"Why, for my country," he said as patriotically as he could manage.

"And not at all for the thrill?" she asked, as she led him past the village, then up away from the beach beyond it.

"Very well," he said with mock chagrin, "it seems you would make a fine spy yourself."

"I would be magnificent," she said with some flourish. "Unfortunately, no one ever asked me."

"Well, if a recommendation is ever requested of me, I will be sure to provide your name," he said, and they shared a smile, all seemingly forgiven.

Soon they entered a wooded area, though it was not at all dense, but filled with greenery and orchid blooms wherever August looked. He couldn't help but stop to take it all in.

"This is beautiful," he said, awestruck, and Iris giggled.

"I told you there was more to see than the shore."

"Do you spend much time here?"

"Not as much as I should," she said, looking around her as though appreciating it herself for the first time. "Marigold loves the outdoors the most of all of us. Daisy had her own secret place somewhere, though she never shared it with any of us. I do enjoy coming this way now and again, the odd time I wish to be alone."

"You do not strike me as a woman who often enjoys such," he said, willing himself to remain serious.

"Not really," she said. "I do enjoy company. I shall show you where I sometimes convene with friends."

He nodded and followed once more, wondering as he did what she meant by 'friends.' They turned around a copse of trees, and in front of them stood a small shack.

"What is this?" he asked, walking around it, while Iris went right to the door.

"I'm not entirely sure why it was originally built," she said. "For hunting, perhaps, or as a small cabin, I have no idea. I'm sure someone in the village would know, but we didn't want to ask for fear someone would come be rid of it. It is rather ghastly."

She was right. The timbers were peeling and some of the boards seemed about to fall out, gaps between some of them now gaping holes. If anything, he would imagine it was likely something of a worry for fire, but Iris seemed fond of it, so he wouldn't voice his concerns.

"What do you use it for?" he asked, wondering if he wanted to know the answer.

"Mostly for when we'd like to speak of things we do not

*An Earl for Iris*

wish others to hear," she said with laughter in her voice and a spark in her eye when she caught his. Suddenly she let out a shocked laugh. "You did not think— oh, but you did." She bit her lip. "I may like to flirt now and again, August, but I am certainly not that type of woman."

Her laughter had quickly faded, and he realized he had insulted her.

"I never said you were."

"But you were thinking it."

"I was not, Iris." Except, he had wondered. "I would be a fool to think such thing of you."

She narrowed her eyes as though she knew he was lying, but then she dropped her head as she scuffed the toe of her half-boot in the grass at her feet. "I have apparently given the wrong impression, for someone such as Ernest Abernathy to think he could take me in the apothecary, or of you wondering such things of me."

"Iris, I—"

"I understand, truly, I do," she said with a sad smile. "It is a lesson for me, I believe."

He sighed. He certainly wasn't going to win this war of words, he realized, nor likely any others to come with her.

"I can, at times, leap to conclusions when I become jealous, Iris."

"You are jealous? Of whom do you have to be jealous?" she asked, spreading her hands out in front of her.

"I'm not entirely sure," he said honestly. "I do not know your past. I only know that you are the most beautiful woman I have ever met, and I desire nothing more than to come to know you better."

She stepped closer to him, raising her hands to the lapels of his jacket.

"What would you like to know?"

"At the moment..." he said with an ache in his chest, "a reminder of what your lips feel like upon mine."

She raised an eyebrow. "I would love to appease you, my lord, but then you may receive the wrong idea of me — that I am a wanton woman."

"I would not," he promised, but she still seemed wary. "Very well," he said with a sigh, "we shall do nothing of the sort. Come, let us return to the inn."

She nodded and they began their walk back in companionable silence. When they neared the village once more, she stopped suddenly and he turned to ask her what was the matter. Before he could get the words out, however, she stood on the tips of her toes and brought her lips to his. After a moment of surprise, warmth flooded through him at not only the sensations her touch evoked but also her enthusiastic approach and the fact that she didn't hesitate to take what she wanted, when she wanted.

She was something, this woman, he thought as she touched her tongue to his lips and he opened to her, to taste her and tease her in turn. He grasped her about the waist, pulling her flush against him, and he determined they were fortunate they had not stopped at that ramshackle building in the woods for it was likely that neither of them would have had the good sense to stop when they should.

It was simply that Iris was too soft, too sensual, and altogether too tempting. He was not a man who easily said no, particularly when the reward far outweighed the risk. And Iris was more reward than he could ever fathom.

He dug his fingers into the soft curls of her hair, feeling tendrils escaping the pins as he did so. He groaned as he pushed her back against one of the trees, hearing her soft yelp into his mouth when she must have come into contact with a sharp branch behind her.

*An Earl for Iris*

One of August's hands began to drift, down the soft fabric of the dress covering the top of her arm, over the skin below it, lower still to the bodice of her dress. He ran his hand over the fabric that covered her ample breasts and would have loosened it to see what was underneath if he hadn't heard a shout from beyond their hiding place.

He broke away from her quickly before realizing it was the sounds of children, likely playing near the water beyond these secluded trees. He looked back to Iris once more, but though she was smiling, the moment was lost, and he inwardly cursed though he knew it was likely fortune looking upon them.

She took his arm, giving it a quick squeeze before they continued to walk once more, though August had difficulty returning to any thoughts but her. Iris Tavners — the daughter of an innkeeper.

Interesting, he hadn't had once thought of Amelia since he and Iris had begun their walk earlier that afternoon. He hadn't questioned her, hadn't wondered if she would betray him as Amelia had.

He was falling in love with this woman. She had his heart — could she take his mind as well?

## 15

Iris hummed a merry tune as she cleaned the floor of the guest dining room. It was not a task she especially enjoyed, but it seemed over the past two days, since she and August had found peace between one another and kissed in the copse, that nothing was as disagreeable as it usually was. She loved him. She could feel it in her very soul, from the top of her head to the tips of her toes.

Oh, she had imagined herself in love before, but now she knew that what she had felt for others had been infatuation. August had captured her heart, and she was determined that before he left, whenever that day came, he would know the extent of her feelings and would take her with him, wherever he must go.

She was so lost in her thoughts that she was startled when the door to the room swung open to reveal Violet and Marigold standing in the entrance.

"Oh!" Iris said, her hand clutching her breast. "My goodness, the two of you startled me."

"I'm so sorry, Iris," Marigold said, and Iris snapped her attention to her sister. It was only then that she noticed the two of them wore matching expressions of pity as they looked down at her, and she quickly stood to face them.

"What is it?" she asked quickly, her eyes flitting from one of them to the other. "Is it Mother? Father? Daisy?"

But no. For then they would be equally as upset instead of standing there looking at her with such sympathy.

"Perhaps we should sit down," Violet said, gesturing to the table, but Iris shook her head impatiently as she flung the rag she was holding down on the floor next to the bucket of soapy water.

"Tell me,' she demanded, ire growing along with her impatience.

Wordlessly, Violet reached into her skirts and pulled a piece of paper out from her pocket. She began to circle it within her fingers, so much so that it took all Iris had within her not to snatch it out of her hand, as Marigold intervened to explain.

"Iris, Lord Westwood has departed."

Iris stared at her sister.

"Pardon me?"

"He left urgently this afternoon. Apparently, he no longer required a room here and left town."

Iris felt her mouth fall open but it was no longer within her power to close it. Suddenly it felt as though her knees were going to buckle, but her sisters were prepared and quickly drew her down to one of the dining chairs.

"He did not... he could not have," she managed, wanting to wipe those stupid expressions of pity off of her sisters' faces.

Marigold placed her hand on Iris' knee.

"Had the two of you... made any promises to one another?"

Of course they hadn't. They had been too busy stealing

kisses and murmuring flirtatious lines. But she couldn't say that to her sisters.

"No," she said, choosing the quick truth instead. "I had thought, however..."

She couldn't finish the sentence, for she realized that whatever she had thought, it had clearly been of her own imaginings. She and August had had their fun, but obviously that was all it was to him — fun. All he had said to her was that he was not interested in a relationship after what had happened to him, that he would not and could not trust her. As much as he had apologized for saying so, never had he declared any other thought.

Tears burned the backs of her eyes, and a lump began to form in her throat. As much as she knew she could be rather prone to hysterics, she didn't want to cry about this, which caused her heart to ache so desperately, in front of anyone — not even her sisters. She gestured to the paper in Violet's hands.

"What is that?"

"He left this for you. I found it in his room when Father sent me to clean it."

Iris wanted to ask how long they had known of this, but did it really matter? He was gone and clearly had no desire to take her with him.

When Iris made no movement to take the paper, Violet placed it down on the table in front of her.

As though sensing her need to be alone, Marigold patted her arm as she rose from the chair next to her.

"We will be outside if you need us, Iris," she said gently. "Please do not hesitate to ask."

Iris nodded mutely and then picked up the note before her.

. . .

*An Earl for Iris*

Iris,

*I greatly enjoyed our time together, but unfortunately, I must now leave Southwold and return to my former life. I apologize I did not have time to say farewell, but an urgent matter arose. I will remember our time together.*

*Yours,*

*August*

SHE FLUNG the paper back down on the table in disgust. That was it? No words of love, no admission of any feelings toward her besides the fact that he had *enjoyed* their time? Well, good riddance to him then. It was the most impersonal note she had ever read, and she picked it up and threw it in the grate. Very well. If that was all she meant to him, then she would relegate him to the very same status in her mind.

She picked up her rag and returned to her task once more, only this time there was no song on her tongue but rather rage in her mind and hurt in her heart as she attacked the floor below her.

∽

AUGUST GRITTED his teeth as he attempted to overcome the pain of the rope as it dug into his wrists while he cursed his own stupidity.

Iris had been right. She would have made a far better spy, for she had intuition — something he clearly lacked.

The light through the gaps of the wall was becoming dimmer, and he wondered how long he would remain tied here, without food or water. Why hadn't the man simply killed him instead of leaving him here alone?

As he began to eventually drift off despite his best efforts, he heard the steady beat of horse's hooves on the ground, which before long were replaced by a man's footsteps on the stairs leading up to the door of his prison.

"Lord Westwood!" Thomas Cooper said, walking in the door as though he was calling upon him in his sitting room. "Did you miss me?"

The man's voice was nearly unrecognizable now as he allowed his natural accent to return, no longer concerned with hiding his identity.

He took the container of water off of his shoulder and chucked it at August, who of course had no capacity to catch it with his arms behind his back. It connected with his stomach before dropping into his lap, and Cooper laughed.

"Ah, *pardon moi*. Allow me to help you, *mon seigneur*."

He laughed again, and August's blood began to run hotly through his veins. He attempted to deny the water when Cooper began to pour it into his mouth, but the man forced his jaw open and practically choked him with it.

Once his coughing abated, August whipped his head up to Cooper.

"What do you want with me?" he seethed. "Why do you not just kill me and be done with it?"

"Now, now, *mon ami*, that would be too much fun. First, you are going to tell me what you know."

"I know nothing," August said bitterly. "You are wasting your time with me. All I did was have my fun in the French court and then return home."

"Come now, do not tell me you were so unsuccessful a spy as that."

"It's true. I was completely inept," August said, narrowing his eyes at the foreigner, most ashamed that his words were true. "Release me, and I will give you time to be gone from here."

"You are quite confusing, Westwood," Cooper said. "Do you want me to kill you or let you go free?"

"I would take the freedom if it's on offer," he said with a shrug, and Cooper laughed.

"A charmer to the end, are you?"

"So it may seem."

"Perhaps what you say is true. For, otherwise, it would not have been so easy for me to overwhelm you, now would it have been?"

"There were two of you."

"But still," Cooper said, raising his hands in surrender. "My less-than-competent partner, Mr. Abernathy, should have been easy enough to overcome."

It was true. August could have taken out Abernathy in but a moment. Cooper and Abernathy, however, had the element of surprise.

Cooper had asked to join August on his walk that morning. He had been subconsciously following a similar trail that he and Iris had taken but the other day when Abernathy had approached from behind, a gun trained on him, and then Cooper had forced him into this shack — the very same one Iris had shown him.

"Well, Lord Westwood, allow me to explain what will happen now," Cooper said. "You will tell me what you know. I was going to return with my tools in order to *persuade* you to do so, but another idea comes to mind. One for which I must thank my new friend, Mr. Abernathy."

It was fear that now began to roil within August.

"I know you appreciate as much as I just how lovely the Tavners sisters are," Cooper said. "It appears that Abernathy also shares that sentiment."

"Cooper, if you—" August began to growl, but the man twirled on his heel and raised a finger in the air between them.

"Comtois, actually," he interrupted. "'Cooper' is so... English. As we were. I shall give you the night to think this through. We must know what you have told your superiors, Westwood, and who they are. If you have nothing to tell us in the morning, well then, it is not you who shall suffer, but your lover and her sister. It would be a shame, wouldn't it?"

August said nothing, though he began to shake with fury and his inability to do anything about the cause of it.

"My apologies. I can see I have upset you. Ah well, the choice is yours. *Bonne nuit, Seigneur* Westwood."

And with one final grin just visible in the nearly absent light, he was gone.

## 16

Iris flung herself backward on her bed.

She had always loved to play the part of a woman scorned, but the truth was now that she truly knew how it felt, it wasn't a position in which she wanted to find herself any longer. For it hurt something awful.

She had been upset when Lord Westwood had returned to London the first time, but she had expected it. This time... this time she had hoped there could be more between them, had been looking for a promise of a life together.

What a fool she had been.

Iris jumped when her door opened, once more revealing her sisters.

"What is the matter with the two of you?" she asked as Marigold's dog, Clover, rushed into the room and jumped on the bed, licking Iris' face. "Do you ever knock?"

"Iris, I must speak with you immediately," Violet said, and only then did Iris note that her sister's cheeks were flushed, her dress untidy, and her hair unkempt. Iris reached out, pulling a twig from her sister's golden-brown hair as she did so.

"Violet, where have you been?"

"That's just it," Violet said hurriedly. "I must tell you of what I have discovered."

"Go on," Iris said, curious despite her current melancholy.

"Well," Violet said, then swallowed hard, her eyes dancing from side to side. "You were right."

"Of course I was," Iris said indignantly, but then paused for a moment before asking, "about what?"

"About Thomas Cooper," Violet said, swaying back and forth from one foot to the other as her hands wrung together nervously. "He is not the man he declares himself to be."

"Aha, I knew it!" Iris said triumphantly, but then her exhilaration fled when she remembered Violet's state. "What did he do to you?" she asked, already standing from the bed, prepared to defend her sister's honor.

"Nothing, he did nothing," Violet said hurriedly. "That is, he did nothing to me."

"But..."

"He has Lord Westwood."

"What?" Iris stared at her incredulously. "Whatever do you mean? And tell the story quickly, Violet, don't make it into a novel."

Marigold frowned at her, but Iris didn't care. She needed to know all that Violet did.

"As much as I didn't want to admit it, your suspicions about him remained on my mind, for you always do have a sense about people," Violet said, twisting her fingers together as she held her hands in front of her. "And when I reflected on it, he did ask a lot of questions about our guests and the comings and goings and who they were. And he was awfully interested in your Lord Westwood."

*An Earl for Iris*

"In August?" Iris repeated, and Violet nodded.

"I overheard the two of them arranging a walk through the woods yesterday morning, and then the very next thing I knew Father was telling us that Lord Westwood had returned home. He only knew because Mr. Cooper had told him so and it seemed unlikely that all would happen so fast, so when Thomas— Mr. Cooper— went out late last night I... well, I followed him."

"Violet!" Marigold and Iris exclaimed at the same time, though Marigold's voice was full of concern while Iris was more impressed than anything.

"You could have been caught!" Marigold said, and while of course she was right, Iris had other concerns at the moment.

"Where did he go?"

"To that old cabin in the woods, just beyond the shore — the one you and your friends like to frequent," she said to Iris, and Iris' eyes widened.

"Mr. Cooper went there?"

"He did," Violet nodded. "I could hear him speaking within. Oh, Iris, Lord Westwood is there, and I believe he is being held captive! When I heard Mr. Cooper speaking, he didn't sound like he normally did."

"What did he sound like?"

"He sounded like a foreigner. I think he spoke some French."

The three of them exchanged looks now as the implications of Violet's words began to sink in.

"He has Lord Westwood," Iris said urgently, "we must go release him."

"It's near midnight," Violet said, her eyes wide, "and Mr. Cooper has returned to the inn."

"We cannot leave August!" Iris exclaimed, but Marigold placed a hand on her arm.

"I understand, Iris, I do, but it will be difficult to find our way in the dark, no matter how well we know the lands. We will leave the moment the sun begins to rise, which is early enough now."

Iris chewed her lip, not happy with the idea but unsure of what else they could do.

"Very well," she sighed. "I shall get prepared as I do not think I shall sleep a wink."

"No one would in this circumstance," Marigold said reassuringly. "I wish Jacob was still here, but he had to return home yesterday to see to a matter."

"That is fine," Iris said confidently, "we can do this ourselves."

"What if there are others nearby who are helping Cooper?"

"And what if we are wrong? We would look like fools chasing after a man who had simply left me behind."

"I believe he's on his own. Who else would help a French spy?" Violet said, and Marigold finally agreed.

Iris sat on her bed as her sisters left, knowing it was going to be a very long night.

∼

Time continued to pass, however, as it always did, and soon enough Iris was dressed and waiting for her sisters downstairs. She heard no other movements in the house despite the number of times she checked to see if she could hear Cooper moving about within the guest quarters.

Soon enough her sisters were down the stairs as well.

They walked in near silence with the backdrop of the

*An Earl for Iris*

rising sun behind them, turning the sky a brilliant pattern of orange, yellow, and pink. But it was difficult to appreciate the scene as Iris' stomach was in turmoil over what lay ahead of them.

And then there was the other aspect to consider — that, if what Violet said was true, August hadn't left her. It also didn't mean that he had chosen to stay with her, for Iris still didn't know his intentions, but he hadn't left without saying goodbye, so perhaps... but that didn't matter. Not now.

She hadn't wanted to think of the possibilities as she sat helpless in her room, but he could be hurt or... worse. The thought sent her heart racing and tears burned her eyes. Iris could hardly fathom the thought of a world without August. He had become too much a part of her heart. Even if he didn't want to be with her, at least knowing that he was somewhere within the world was much better than the thought that he could be... gone.

As branches slapped against her, Iris shook her head and blinked her tears away rapidly. She couldn't think like that — not now. Not when August was likely alone in that shack, waiting whatever fate had in store for him.

She pushed on, more determined than ever to save him and tell him just exactly how she felt.

∽

August heard a thump from outside the door of the hunting shack, and he braced himself. He was so close to fraying the rope that bound his hands together. He had found an old nail protruding from one of the walls, and had scraped up his hands as he had spent the night backed against it, moving the rope up and down as he attempted to free himself.

With one last great surge, he pulled his hands apart with as much force as he possibly could, and the rope finally snapped. He rubbed at his raw wrists, but as much as they pained him, the freedom had never felt so wonderful.

He stood beside the door, prepared to tackle whoever came through it. He wished there was a window in this damn little cabin, but as it was, he had, at least, the element of surprise. August heard footsteps begin to climb the steps, and he grew worried as he realized there was more than one set.

The door flung open and August launched himself toward the arrivals to attack. As he began to fall to the floor with the first body, however, he had to turn in mid-air, for he realized that this was certainly not Comtois nor any of his men. No, this was not a man at all, but rather—

"Iris?" he cried out in shock as they landed in a heap on the floor, she thankfully on top of him. "What the hell are you doing here?"

"That is hardly the way to address your rescuer," she said indignantly as she stood, and he nearly laughed in spite of the situation.

"My rescuer?"

"Yes, well, along with my sisters," she said, gesturing beyond him, and he turned to see Marigold and Violet standing at the door. He nodded to them.

"Ladies."

"Lord Westwood, whatever happened here?" Marigold asked, but he shook his head.

"There will be time for that later. Come, we must—"

"Well, well, what do we have here?"

They all turned nearly as one to see that Comtois was striding up the steps now, a pistol outstretched in his hand, which he pointed at each of them in turn.

*An Earl for Iris*

"It is truly a fête now, is it not? *Bonjour,* Violet, *mon amour.*"

He reached out as though to stroke her cheek and Violet recoiled away from him, her face twisted into one of disgust.

"Ah, *ma petite* Violet, you truly thought I was interested in you, did you not? You should have listened to your sister when she told you I was not to be trusted. But, alas, here you are, about to succumb to the same fate as the rest of them. If you were a different woman, Miss Iris, you would have believed the note I left for you. But alas, you would never believe a man would leave you, could you? You ladies should not have left the comfort of your inn. Trust me, Lord Westwood is not worth it."

"It's true," August said, walking over to Comtois and standing in front of his pistol so that Iris and her sisters were shielded. "You shouldn't have come, Iris. None of you should have."

Iris looked pained at his words.

"I would come for you, August, over and over again, regardless of the outcome."

He looked back at her over his shoulder, blinking away the sudden prick of tears at her words. He managed a weak smile before returning to Comtois.

"Let them go," he said. "They are not what you came here for."

"They know too much," he said. "Unfortunately, their fate is sealed."

He cocked the hammer of the gun, lifted it to August's head, and smiled.

## 17

August held Comtois' gaze, doing all he could to keep his attention as Iris slowly rounded to the other side of the Frenchman. He had no idea just what she was planning to do, but he had to trust her — and he did. He could hardly believe that she and her sisters had come after him — alone. Perhaps not the best idea, but brave, nonetheless. What kind of women were these?

"I have one last request," August said.

"Very well," answered Comtois, "this should be interesting."

"It is, I promise you that," said August. It took everything in him to not look in Iris' direction but he could sense her movement.

He cleared his throat. "As it is, I would like—"

*Smack* came the sound of a piece of wood — one he hadn't noticed in the dim light, but then, she knew this place far better than he did — connecting with the back of Comtois' head. He tumbled to the floor as Iris looked at August with a huge smile of satisfaction on her face.

"That should do it," she said.

*An Earl for Iris*

August had no words. He crossed to her in two large steps, rounding the unconscious Comtois, took Iris' face within his hands, and kissed her long and hard. He heard her sisters gasp and giggle slightly behind him, but he didn't care whatsoever as he plundered her lips and her soft, enthusiastic mouth with his.

A sound arose behind him, but it took August a moment longer than it should have to register. Fortunately, the Tavners sisters were quicker than he was, and Violet had scooped up the pistol in her hand.

Ernest Abernathy walked through the door, and August was shocked to see that he was not alone.

"Ridlington?" he said, puzzled, as one of the other boarders appeared behind Abernathy, whose hands were tied and a knife held at his back.

"Lord Westwood," said the tall man, who tilted his hat back to look at them all. "Glad to see you are all right."

"What are you doing here?" August asked.

"General Dobbins sent me to Southwold to look out for you," he said. "Though it seems these women did my job for me... I found this fellow was approaching the cabin, ready to assist your French friend here."

"Why?" Iris demanded, her disgust growing as she looked at Abernathy. "While you have the worst character of anyone I know, I never would have thought you to be a traitor to your country."

"It wasn't my country," Ernest sneered. "What mattered was taking out the fancy lord who had stolen your affections. I am nobody's fool."

"You are your own fool," Iris said, turning her nose up at him, and August loved her all the more for it.

"We'll take these two back to town and find somewhere to leave them until we can summon additional help from the Crown," Ridlington said. "If that works for you, Westwood."

"Absolutely," August said, shaking the man's hand. "Away we go."

It was quite the party that arrived in Southwold and many of the villagers emerged to watch them walk by, as though they were a parade marching through. Violet looked like she wanted to hide, but Iris seemed was clearly enjoying herself. August could only smile. He reached over and quickly squeezed her hand before securing their prisoners in the stable, though he couldn't wait until he would see her again.

~

Iris had never been more thankful for Marigold.

The family was seated around their sitting room, discussing all that had occurred. Their father was livid, their mother beside herself.

Marigold was, thankfully, a calming presence, and had managed to have the family sit down to discuss all that had happened in a rational manner.

Only now that they knew all, their parents were once again becoming upset.

"How could those men involve women — my daughters! — in such activities? It's unheard of. I am shocked. Shocked, I tell you! Although," Elias grumbled, not looking any of them in the eye, "I am rather proud of all of you as well."

Iris smiled wide until their mother began again.

"You could have been injured — or worse!" She wrung her hands together. "What would we have done if something had happened to you?"

*An Earl for Iris*

"Hired more maids?" Iris said wryly, which only caused tears to begin to run down her mother's face.

"Is that what you think, that we only care about you in regard to your work around here? Oh, Iris, we love you all so much, and couldn't bear it if anything were to happen to you!"

"Mother," she said, tears beginning to form in her own eyes, chagrined at her hasty words. "I'm sorry."

Her mother moved in to embrace her, and soon enough the three sisters and their mother were all hugging and crying.

"I wish Daisy were here!" Alice said, and Iris stepped back, wiping the tears.

"Soon enough, she will come to visit," Iris said. "Not to worry."

"I know," Alice replied, her voice watery. "It's just... my girls are all marrying and going away, and as happy as I am, I didn't realize how sad I would be as well."

"I'm still here, Mother," Violet said before her voice turned heated. "And it seems I likely will be for a very long time, for the only man who seemed interested in me was a French spy who was using me for information. Oh, how could I be so stupid?"

"You are not stupid, Violet," Iris said firmly. "He was trained to do such a thing. I'm sure you are not the first who was so captivated by a handsome man with sweet words and charm. I have certainly been a victim of such as well."

"But Lord Westwood loves you!" Violet protested, her words now capturing the attention of their parents as well.

"Lord Westwood?" her father said, his chest puffing out now. "Well, then. Another lord for my daughters!"

"I'm not so sure," Iris said. "I may have just been a diversion to his boredom here, and that is all."

"I don't think so," Marigold said with a soft smile. "In fact, I think he just may have something to say to you."

She nodded toward the door, and they all looked up to see August standing in the doorframe, a smile on his face, but his weight was shifting back and forth between his feet as though he was awkwardly intruding.

"Come in, son," Elias said, causing Iris to cringe, and August stepped in the door.

"I apologize for any danger I brought onto your family, Mr. Tavners," he said. "I had been assured my identity would be safe here, but apparently I was followed from London. It seems I don't make much of a spy."

"Nonsense," Iris' father said. "I made the arrangement with the Crown, so I was well aware who was coming to the inn and what the consequences might be."

August nodded, though he still seemed upset.

"General Dobbins will be arriving in a day or two to see to the prisoners," he said. "Then all will be out of your way."

"And you?" Iris couldn't help but ask, "will you be going as well?"

"That remains to be seen," he responded. "Would you... would you walk with me for a moment, Iris?"

"Of course," she said, her heart beating rapidly as she rose. She felt her family's gazes upon her but didn't say anything as August took her arm and they walked out of the room.

"Let's go outdoors," Iris said. "I could use some air."

They stepped outside onto the sand, and as soon as they were out of eyesight of any window, August abruptly pulled her close against him.

"My God, Iris," he said. "I can hardly believe what you did. When I saw that gun trained on you..."

He closed his eyes and leaned his forehead in against

*An Earl for Iris*

hers. She placed her hands on his chest, her fingers gripping his shirt.

"I could hardly bear to think of what I would do were anything to happen to you."

He took her face within his broad fingers and leaned back, his warm brown eyes boring into hers. She bit her lip and blinked.

"I know I haven't been good to you, Iris. I looked you over for another woman, I didn't trust you for no fault of your own. And yet you remained with me, you believed in me, you gave me another chance. You risked your life for me. You are the most amazing woman I have ever met. You do what you feel is best for other people, you speak your mind, and nothing frightens you. Iris... I do not know what kind of life I am going to lead or what I have to offer you. I have no idea if I will have the ability to return home, or if I must go into hiding somewhere else. But I must ask... will you go with me? Will you wait for me if you must?"

His eyes were pleading as he looked at her, but he had nothing to fear.

"Of course I will," she said, a grin spreading on her face. "I will wait for you as long as I must, August, I promise you that, and it means more than anything that you trust me enough to ask. But August, I will come with you wherever and whenever that may be, in whatever life we have to lead together. I love you, August Williams, and I cannot imagine life without you. For a moment when I thought I might have to, I... I simply couldn't bear it. There is no other man for me but you."

The smile spread on his face as she spoke, and now he began to laugh, a low laugh that warmed her to her very soul. He leaned in and kissed her now, a kiss she felt radiate throughout her body.

"I love you, Iris Tavners," he said, taking a moment to lean back away from her, "will you be my wife?"

"Yes," she breathed, "a thousand times yes."

And the kiss they then shared was one of the promise of all that the future held for them.

## 18

The General arrived the very next day. He looked very regal riding into Southwold, a town that was now becoming used to a wide array of military figures visiting them. The stables became an interrogation room of sorts, and while Iris' father told his daughters to stay far from the military men, Iris, of course, couldn't help herself.

She snuck in the back door and found the stall of one of her family's horses, Sally.

"Hi, girl," she said as the horse gave a whinny, "don't tell anyone I'm here."

She settled herself in the straw, where she had to make herself comfortable, for it was a long wait until anything of importance was revealed.

Comtois was not a particularly strong man, and when he was offered the chance for a lighter sentence, he quickly turned over all of the information the English wanted from him. As far as he was aware, only one other man, his superior, knew anything about August's true identity. Ernest was nothing more than a bitter man seeking revenge, and the General cared little about him.

After the interrogation, the military men left to discuss the situation in Elias' study, which Iris, unfortunately, no longer had any access to, so instead, she had to wait with Violet in their own sitting room as Marigold had returned home.

"Well, I have some news," August said as he entered the room and took a seat next to Iris. She reached between them and squeezed his hand, which he responded to with a small side smile just for her. "Fortunately, it seems that Comtois was one of only a few men who knew of my identity. The General has commissioned a special team to ensure that those who are aware of who I truly am will be taken care of. Once that mission is over, I will be able to return home, but in the meantime... here I will stay, as will Ridlington for added protection."

He returned Iris' hand squeeze.

"On that note," he looked around at her family before his gaze stopped on her father. He lifted his hand, joined with Iris', onto his lap. "I would like to marry Iris, as soon as possible, if you are in agreement. We would stay here as long as we must before we would return to London and my estate. I have not yet acted as Earl, but I'm sure with Iris, I can do anything — or she will do it for me."

"Well, of course, my boy!" Elias said, and Iris cringed at how he addressed August, but he didn't seem to mind. "I'll speak with the minister."

"Very well," August said with a smile, and Iris didn't think she had ever before felt such contentment as she did in this moment.

*An Earl for Iris*

NOT UNTIL, as it were, three weeks later, when she and August faced one another at the foot of her bed.

She grinned at her husband. He grinned back. She took a step toward him. He followed suit. Iris wasn't sure who moved first, but in the next moment, they were flush against one another, then falling back on the bed behind them.

The passion they had stored inside for so long poured out as now, finally, they were able to take all that they felt for one another and act upon it. August's hands seemed to be everywhere, his lips trailing along behind their path. The dress she had worn for the ceremony — her Sunday best — was soon over her head and on the floor, her chemise quickly joining it.

Iris had a bit more difficulty with the layers of August's clothes, but he was happy to lend a hand.

And when it came time for them to truly join together, while the passion was still present, he gently loved her as truly and tenderly as she could ever imagine.

"I suppose this isn't quite the comfort that you are used to," Iris said afterward with a bit of a smile as she looked around the interior of her bedroom. She had shared it with Violet for so many years, until Daisy and Marigold moved out and Violet left for their room.

It was the room of her childhood, with her mother's discarded floral paintings on the walls, a worn blanket on the bed, and a mattress that sagged slightly in the middle. She had always hated how much it did so when she and Violet would constantly fight to keep from rolling into one another, but with August beside her, she didn't much mind.

"I far prefer the company here," he said, brushing his hand over her hair before twirling one of her curls around his finger.

She smiled. "Will your mother be awfully upset, that she wasn't here for the ceremony?"

"Oh yes," he said drolly, "so much so that we will likely have to have another wedding when we return to London. Would that be all right with you?"

"I would marry you every day," she said, and he answered her with a kiss.

"And what about our marriage night?"

"I suppose we could repeat that, too," she said with a wink.

"As you wish," he said, and when he kissed her again, it was one that promised his love forever more.

∼

**THE END**

∼

*Sign-up for Ellie's email list and "Unmasking a Duke," a regency romance, will come straight to your inbox — free!*

www.prairielilypress.com/ellies-newsletter/

You will also receive links to giveaways, sales, updates, launch information, promos, and the newest recommended reads.

# THE DUKE SHE WISHED FOR

## HAPPILY EVER AFTER BOOK 1

PREVIEW
Begin the Happily Ever After series with the story of Tabitha and Nicholas...

# CHAPTER 1

The creak of the shop's front door opening floated through the heavy curtains that separated Tabitha's workshop from the sales floor. She tensed over the silk ribbon she was attempting to fashion into a flower shape and waited for the sound of her stepsister Frances to greet whoever had just walked into the Blackmore Milliner shop.

She paused, waiting a little bit longer before pushing out a frustrated breath and standing. These velvet ribbon flowers she had learned to fashion were part of the reason Blackmore hats sat atop some of the finest female heads in polite society — she had a knack for creating new ways to adorn the same old bonnet or beaver hat styles so that a woman of a certain class stood out among her peers.

This ability was both a blessing and a curse, it turned out. Her creativity meant Tabitha brought customers through the front door, to the shop she and her father had built after her mother died when she was seven years old. It had brought Tabitha and her father, the baronet Elias Blackmore, closer together in their time of immeasurable grief, and the shop had flourished.

The relationship between father and daughter remained strong, and when she was twelve years of age, he approached her and told her he wanted to marry a baroness from the North Country. The baroness had a daughter about her own age, he'd added. Tabitha had been happy for her father and excited at the prospect of having a sister. She had welcomed her new family with an open heart and open arms.

What a silly little fool she'd been, Tabitha thought with derisive snort as she pushed herself to her feet and through the brocade curtains to greet the newcomer. Lord only knew where Frances had gone off to. Likely shopping with her mother, Ellora.

Upon the untimely death of Sir Elias Blackmore three years after the marriage, Tabitha had been utterly devastated. Lady Blackmore, however, hadn't wasted much time in putting Tabitha in her place. No longer the family's most cherished daughter, Tabitha had been shoved into the workroom and largely ignored, but for her skills as a milliner — they kept just enough of her stepmother's attention on her.

The more she stood up to Ellora, the more her stepmother threatened to throw her out on the street. Knowing it was within Ellora's nature to follow through on her threat, Tabitha did her best to ignore and avoid her stepmother, focusing instead on her work and her ambitions.

It was better, Tabitha supposed, than staying in their townhome all day long worrying about social calls that never came or invitations that would never arrive. The family name had suffered greatly under Lady Blackmore and Miss Frances Denner, her daughter from a previous marriage.

In truth, Tabitha was little more than a servant with no money to speak of, no family to lean on, and no real prospects other than her creations on which to pin her hopes of ever escaping the lot she'd been given after her father died.

In the showroom, Tabitha scanned the floor in search of the new arrival. It took a moment, but her eyes finally landed on a small, older man in a fine suit. He had a slip of paper in his hand, and he approached Tabitha with the air of someone who didn't waste time.

"Good afternoon, Miss," the man began with perfect, practiced speech. "My name is Mr. McEwan. I serve as the steward in the house of Her Grace the Duchess of Stowe. I have a receipt for a series of hats I believe she had ordered, and she is requesting that they be delivered tomorrow afternoon."

Tabitha felt her stomach sink. If this was the order she was thinking of, the one currently on her worktable, there was no way under the stars that the three hats would be ready by tomorrow. She was only one flower (out of seven) into the first bonnet, and it was a slow process to convince the requested velvet ribbon to behave.

"I am sorry, sir," she began, trying to get his eyes off the wilder ostrich-plumed hats next to her and back on her. "That is almost four days before we agreed upon. I'm certain there is no feasible way the work can be done, and done well, by tomorrow."

That got the older man's attention. He huffed, turned a bit pink around the cheeks, and sputtered.

"There is simply no choice, my dear," he said abruptly but not unkindly. "His Grace is arriving home from his trip to France early and therefore the parties his mother has planned for him will be adjusted accordingly. And so, her wardrobe *must* be ready — she said so herself. She is willing to pay handsomely for your ability to expedite the process."

Tabitha drew in a breath at that and considered. She was having such a difficult time scrimping a small savings together to buy herself a seat at the Paris School of Millinery that this "bonus" money might perhaps get her there that much quicker. Assuming, of course, that Ellora didn't catch wind of the extra earnings. She was quick to snatch up all but the barest pennies.

Tabitha closed her eyes for a moment and drew a steadying breath. If she worked through the night and her needle and thread held true, there was a *slight* chance that she could finish in time. She said so to Mr. McEwan, who beamed brightly at her.

"I knew it," he said with a laugh. "I have faith you Miss — er, I apologize, I did not hear your name?"

Tabitha sighed.

"Tabitha Blackmore," she said, noticing how quickly he'd changed the subject on her. "I did not exactly say that I would be able to—"

She was cut off again by Mr. McEwan, who gave her a slight bow and provided directions to the home of the Dowager Duchess of Stowe on the other side of the city.

"I shall see you tomorrow, then, my dear," he said with a quick grin. "Be sure to pack a bag to stay at least one evening, maybe two. I am certain Her Grace's attendants will need proper coaching on how best to pair the hats. You will be paid, of course!"

With that the short man with wisps of white hair on his head that stood up like smoke was gone, disappearing into the streets of Cheapside.

Tabitha leaned back against the counter behind her and blew out a breath, a little overwhelmed at the entire encounter.

On the one hand, she had found a way to increase her

savings and take a step closer to the education her father had wanted for her. On the other, getting through the night in one piece was not guaranteed. She would have to return to the shop after dinner and do so without rousing Lady Blackmore's suspicions, which would not be easy.

Tabitha kicked at a crushed crepe ribbon flower that hadn't been tossed out properly. Another evening down the back drainpipe it was, then.

"Time away from the witch, I suppose," she muttered as she returned to her worktable, a new fire of inspiration lit beneath her.

∼

Dinner was more complicated than usual, thanks to the fact that Ellora, Tabitha's stepmother, was having one of her *moods*. They could be brought on by anything — the weather (too foul or too pleasant), the noisy street they lived on, memories of her life when she was the daughter of an earl and had endless opportunities for money and titles, or even an egg that had too much salt.

Today's mood, however, had more to do with the fact that her daughter Frances had been recently snubbed. Officially, Ellora was considered a member of the *ton* and her daughter's first season the previous year had nearly cost them the roof over their heads. However, Frances was an ill-tempered, sharp-tongued girl who did little to ensure repeat invitations to dances and parties.

"A true-and-true witch," their housekeeper, Alice, called her. Alice was the only servant left on staff besides Katie, the lady's maid Ellora and Frances shared, so it was up to both Alice and Tabitha to make sure that meals were made and rooms were kept clean. Being an indentured servant in her own home was trying enough, but much worse was having to tidy the room that once held every memento of her father's. It was now completely devoid of every memory of him.

It was as though Baronet Elias Blackmore had never existed. No portraits. No personal belongings. Nothing but the small locket he'd given Tabitha when she was nine years old, which she still wore around her neck.

This evening's dinner was a morose affair, and Tabitha sat silently while Ellora ranted and raved about the social snub of her angel, Frances.

Tabitha looked across the table at her stepsister. Frances was very pretty, she'd give her that much. But her mouth was drawn thin and her blue eyes were more steely than pleasant. Frances had brown hair that one could call more dishwater in color than brunette. However, Ellora spent high sums of money on beauty products and bits and bobs for Katie to fashion Frances' hair into something resembling high fashion each day.

Frances was pouting into her soup while her mother railed beside her. When she glanced up and caught Tabitha looking at her, she scowled.

Tabitha quickly looked away, but Frances jumped on the opportunity to take the attention off her.

"I saw a servant go into the shop this afternoon when I was returning from tea with Adela," Frances said to her mother, her flinty eyes on Tabitha, who inwardly groaned.

So much for secrecy.

Ellora paused in her ranting and raised an eyebrow at her.

"Who was it?"

The words were clipped, and her nose was high in the air while she peered along it at Tabitha.

"A servant for the Dowager Duchess of Stowe," Tabitha replied. "He came to inquire about an order the Duchess sent over a week ago."

It wasn't exactly a lie and it helped her corroborate her story because Ellora had already received the money sent over for the original order.

"And was the order ready?"

Tabitha swallowed hard. She wasn't in the clear yet.

"Almost," she said and lowered her eyes to take a sip of the soup as she inwardly seethed.

"Unacceptable," her stepmother ground out between her teeth. "You lazy, no-good hanger-on. It is no wonder your father's ridiculous hat shop is dying off. He had the laziest cow this side of the river working behind the curtains."

She banged a fist on the table, making Frances jump.

"You get up from this table and you finish that order right this instant." Ellora pointed a long bony finger in the direction of the door, ending Tabitha's dinner before she had progressed past the soup. Tabitha's stomach rumbled in protest, and her fists clenched beneath the table as she longed to tell Ellora what she really thought, but Tabitha knew this was a gift. She would nab a roll from Alice later.

"I am going to stop by in the morning to check your ledger and work progress to make certain you are being completely honest with me," Ellora announced. "And woe be to you if I find that you have been neglecting your work and you have a backlog of orders."

In reality, Tabitha was of legal age and the threats should be harmless. But she was also lacking any real money, any job prospects, and had no titles her father could have passed down to her. Running her father's milliner shop was the closest thing she would have to freedom for the near future, and it would be much better for her if she allowed Ellora the illusion of control for the time being, since the dreadful woman had inherited the shop upon her father's death.

Ellora's threat put Tabitha in a bind. She was due at the Duchess' estate first thing in the morning. As it stood, she'd have to have those pieces done, as well as the other orders on her workbench before then. She closed her eyes and blew out a heavy breath.

It was going to be a very long night.

~

*The Duke She Wished For* is now available for purchase on Amazon, and is free to read through Kindle Unlimited.

# ALSO BY ELLIE ST. CLAIR

*Standalone*

Unmasking a Duke

Christmastide with His Countess

*Happily Ever After*

The Duke She Wished For

Someday Her Duke Will Come

Once Upon a Duke's Dream

He's a Duke, But I Love Him

Loved by the Viscount

Because the Earl Loved Me

Happily Ever After Box Set Books 1-3

Happily Ever After Box Set Books 4-6

*Searching Hearts*

Duke of Christmas

Quest of Honor

Clue of Affection

Hearts of Trust

Hope of Romance

Promise of Redemption

Searching Hearts Box Set (Books 1-5)

*The Unconventional Ladies*

Lady of Mystery

Lady of Fortune

Lady of Providence

Lady of Charade

*Blooming Brides*

A Duke for Daisy

A Marquess for Marigold

An Earl for Iris

## ABOUT THE AUTHOR

Ellie has always loved reading, writing, and history. For many years she has written short stories, non-fiction, and has worked on her true love and passion -- romance novels.

In every era there is the chance for romance, and Ellie enjoys exploring many different time periods, cultures, and geographic locations. No matter when or where, love can always prevail. She has a particular soft spot for the bad boys of history, and loves a strong heroine in her stories.

She enjoys walks under the stars with her own prince charming, as well as spending time at the lake with her children, and running with her Husky/Border Collie cross.

www.prairielilypress.com/ellie-st-clair
ellie@prairielilypress.com

Printed in Great Britain
by Amazon